I LOVE YOU YOU S'MORE

ALSO BY
AURIANE DESOMBRE

FOR YOUNG ADULTS
I Think I Love You

FOR MIDDLE GRADERS
The Sister Split

I LOVE YOU S'MORE

AURIANE DESOMBRE

Delacorte
Romance

Text copyright © 2025 by Auriane Desombre
Cover art copyright © 2025 by Jeff Östberg

Golden sunset over mountains by Johnster Designs used under
license for stock.adobe.com

All rights reserved. Published in the United States by Delacorte Romance,
an imprint of Random House Children's Books, a division of
Penguin Random House LLC, 1745 Broadway, New York, NY 10019.

Delacorte Romance and the colophon are trademarks
of Penguin Random House LLC.

GetUnderlined.com

Educators and librarians, for a variety of teaching tools,
visit us at RHTeachersLibrarians.com

Library of Congress Cataloging-in-Publication Data is available upon request.
ISBN 978-0-593-80754-5 (trade pbk.) — ISBN 978-0-593-80756-9 (ebook)

The text of this book is set in 11.5-point Adobe Garamond Pro.

Editor: Kelsey Horton
Cover Designer: Trisha Previte
Interior Designer: Megan Shortt
Production Editor: Colleen Fellingham
Managing Editor: Tamar Schwartz
Production Manager: Tim Terhune

Printed in the United States of America
1st Printing
First Edition

The authorized representative in the EU for product safety and compliance is
Penguin Random House Ireland, Morrison Chambers, 32 Nassau Street,
Dublin D02 YH68, Ireland. https://eu-contact.penguin.ie

For Sammy, the best dog.

For Eros and Luke, both the best dog.

For Ella and Cali and Chloe and Daphne and Bella and Gunner and Foxy and Timur and Wally and Winston and Rascal and Fiona and Hercules and Phoebe and Bear—all, the best dog.

And for your dog, too. Please tell them they are the best dog, and I love them, and there is nothing in the world so good as the way they see it.

TeleFanHour [21 hours ago]: breaking news!! Sources have confirmed that Allyson Hendricks has called it quits with her high school sweetheart. The pair started dating a year before Allyson was cast as our favorite space exile. We can't help but wonder if the on-screen chemistry with Becca Wallis has anything to do with their recent split . . . #TelephoneHour

Liked by AnneMarieSlate and 71,848 others
View all 21,809 comments

SammyTheBadDog: you KNOW it does. I've shipped BecAlly since their first comic con interview

ABCece: my faith in love is dead

MarlyAndrews: SAMEEEEE

WhereIsPepper: ngl speculating about the dating lives of real, actual people sort of gives me the ick. Her poor ex must be so heartbroken

JuliePeterson: sending so much love to Allyson

KatieKat89: "on-screen" chemistry my ass. It POPS off-screen too!! they were 1000000% holding hands under the table during that promo for the next season!! Our ship is FINALLY SAILING

NatalieWaters: at the end of the day we just want to see Allyson happy. nothing but love to Ally, and her ex too

SandyBecks: Ally is so not okay i can see the pain in her eyes . . . stay strong!! We are here for you!!

LacyMills: #TEAMBECALLY FOREVER

I USED TO BE NAMED IVY, AND I USED TO BE IN LOVE.

Now I'm just carsick, and the whole world has forgotten I even have a name.

The mountain road is made of spiked curves and sharp twists all the way up. The horizon dips and weaves with every jolt of the car. It's a lot for a digestive system that can't even handle gluten.

It doesn't help that I can't take my eyes off my phone. I've been in a free-fall scroll through the entire internet since our lunch stop, when the news broke. It's a miracle I made it a whole week, nursing my tattered heart in the peace of anonymity, but now everyone knows, and everyone with an internet connection is free to air their hot take about my first-ever breakup. I haven't had the courage to read the actual press release yet, but the fan reactions feel like poking a bruise. Swaths of people with fandom profile pictures have been renaming me all morning.

Allyson Hendricks's ex-girlfriend.
Former middle school sweetheart.
That girl in the way of our ship.
Her ex.
Her ex.
Her ex.

Whoever doles out Social Media Main Character of the Day assignments has some serious explaining to do.

From her car seat in front of me, Georgianna lets out a massive shriek. She's only eighteen months old, so she's allowed to do that. I tried earlier, when Dad's car started its slow wind up the San Bernardino Mountains, but it was frowned upon. Natalie shifts in the front seat to pat Georgianna's squat legs.

"We're almost there, Georgie," she says. "I know it's a lot of turns."

"It sure is," mutters Lacey, my older sister.

Natalie gives her an apologetic smile, and Lacey shoots me a knowing glance. Natalie and Dad got married lightning fast after our parents' divorce, and she's convinced we hate her as a result. We don't hate her, but we do accept her attempts to buy our love via takeout and coddly parenting.

"We're not almost there," Dad mumbles. He's scared of heights, and he's been darting glares at the ravine that plunges down one side of the road, peppered with pine trees that bury the horizon. "Which means it's not too late to back out."

That last bit is directed at me, so I roll my eyes. "It's definitely too late to back out."

"Reception is gone," Lacey says, tossing her phone aside.

3

"No it isn't." Tara, who used to be the baby of the family before Georgie, has the back of her phone pressed against the window. "Wait. Yes it is."

As if to prove her point, Georgie lets out another wail. Nugget, curled in the cramped space under Georgie's dangling legs, throws his little puppy head back and joins in.

"You can always back out," Dad says, raising his voice above the chaos of our family as Lacey fumbles through the diaper bag in search of a fresh pacifier. "Especially in light of . . . recent events."

Lacey tilts her head back, trying to catch my gaze again from her perch next to Georgie in the middle row of the family minivan we had to get when we became a four-kid family. I turn my attention back to the window, even though any hope I had of horizon staring curing my nausea has been buried by the pines. *Recent events*—which has been Dad's second-favorite euphemism for my unceremonious dumping, after "The, well, um, you know . . ."—have nothing to do with anything. Dad has been trying to get me to back out of being a camp counselor since he found out that my new summer job coincides with our yearly family camping trip.

Of course, that's one of the major appeals for this job. That and the fact that I finally get to go back to my childhood theater camp. I haven't seen these pines since sixth grade. They haven't changed at all, like they've been keeping watch over this place for me in my absence. But I'd have taken a job rowing a small boat across the Atlantic Ocean in the middle of hurricane season to get out of camping with my family. They're just all so . . .

4

outdoorsy. They frolic up hikes to remote camping grounds, never noticing that I'm always half a mile behind them, gasping for air like my veins are drying up under my skin.

Last year my tent concaved under the weight of unforecasted rain that flooded my sleeping bag. Soggy sleeping bag is not a hell I'd wish on anyone. Not on my stepdad, who I've only met one time, at my mom's wedding. Not on Rynn Walsh, who ditched me in the most dramatic way possible for a sixth grader, right before we moved from LA to San Francisco. Not even on Ally, even though she dumped me out of absolutely *nowhere.*

I was already jumping at the chance to work at my old summer camp. When I saw that the dates would eat right into Dad's campground booking, I called Ms. Patricia, the camp director, and begged her to hire me. Phone calls are my absolute nemesis, so that's really saying something. She remembered me and hired me on the spot. Boom, no camping. Welcome to my summer of making money and pretending I've never even heard of Allyson Hendricks.

"I'm not backing out," I tell Dad. "Besides, do you really want to make a U-turn on this road?"

He sighs but lets it go.

The road thins ahead of us, the curves sharpening so that even though I know exactly where I'm going, I can't see more than a few feet ahead of me. My knuckles whiten as I grip the edge of my seat, fingertips digging into the cushion. I didn't inherit Dad's vertigo, but the twisting heights are enough to get to me, and the nausea bubbles in my throat.

Lacey looks back at me again, forcing me to dodge her eye

contact. She's been doing that a lot in the past week. In light of *recent events*. But I don't want to go through this. It's just something that happened. It doesn't need to define my summer. It happened. It was a dark moment—a soul-crushingly alone moment. But the *moment* has passed. It's over. Moving on.

Mercifully, Natalie was right, and we pull up Camp Acorn Hill's driveway before my stomach has time to turn itself completely inside out. The car lurches to a halt, and the entire Raines-Hymond clan tumbles out of the side door.

The still-familiar sound of a golf cart whirring spins me around, and I smile in spite of myself when I spot Ms. Patricia. I planned to be professional—to prove myself at first glance as a true counselor-ready employee, my camper days behind me—but instead I launch myself at her as soon as she gets her ancient golf cart to stop. Broccoli, her dog, pounces at my knees, his paws dancing against my legs.

"How have you not replaced this thing yet?" I ask, straight into her ear, not ready to let the hug end yet. "Or at least fixed the brakes?"

"That's what I hired you for," Ms. Patricia says.

I can hear her smile, but I'm still hugging her too tightly to see it for myself. Ms. Patricia has a knack for knowing exactly how long a hug needs to last. When Mom dropped me off in the summer before sixth grade, Ms. Patricia let me hug her for almost six minutes straight. She may not have known yet that my parents were kicking off their divorce proceedings that afternoon, but she knew how long that hug had to be. If I'd known that was to be my last summer at Acorn Hill, the hug would've never ended.

Now I'm sure she knows why I need this hug. The whole world knows. She lets me sink into her wide-set shoulders, and keeps her arms in a tight squeeze until I pull away.

"If it's my job to fix the brakes, that thing'll never stop again," I say as I clap my palms against my thighs, inviting Broccoli to leap onto me. He takes me up on it, his paws leaving dirt tracks along the hem of my floral skirt as I ruffle his fur. Nugget, dangling from the car window, gives a jealous yelp. Which is probably exactly what I sounded like every time Ally ditched me to hang out with her costars. I cringe at the thought.

"This is where we leave you," Dad says. "Unless . . ."

"It's too late to turn back, Dad," I say, looking over my shoulder. He already has his hiking boots on so he doesn't have to waste a second between parking the car and launching himself up the nearest trail. It's not a summer plan I fit into. Not like here. Acorn Hill still has a place carved out for me. The wind whistling through the pine needles might as well be carrying my extremely off-key sixth-grade rendition of "On the Steps of the Palace" from the first act–only production of *Into the Woods* that concluded my last summer here.

"It definitely is," Ms. P says. "I need you. We're understaffed this year as it is."

Dad laughs. "All I'm hearing is the working conditions will be bad," he whispers as he leans in to hug me.

At least the working conditions come with functional

showers and easy access to gluten-free bread, which is more than his vacation conditions can say. The "gluten-free bun" on the burger at Dad's favorite diner is so crunchy it might as well be a corn chip.

This feels like a good place to clarify that I have actual celiac disease. I am not one of those LA people who refuses to eat bread lest it give me a pimple. Those people are my absolute nemeses. They have given me and the other gluten intolerants who frequent findmeglutenfree.com such a bad name. My worst fear is having to explain this to waiters lest they judge me.

Well, that and the haunting, omnipresent void of loneliness staring back at me since the breakup. But those two are basically tied for first place.

Dad lets me go, his eyes already trained back on the car, his trip, and the family members who actually want to go. All of them but me. I ignore the way that stings as I wave goodbye to Lacey. She wiggles her fingers at me as she rebuckles her seat belt, but Georgie wails midwave, and she drops her hand to tend to her.

"See you in a few weeks," Natalie coos from the front seat, with too much verve in her voice, trying to make up for Dad's lack of enthusiasm at my gainful employment. "Have the best time."

They pull away, the car rattling down the winding driveway, and even though I asked for this, the moment still sticks in my throat, and I have to swallow hard to dislodge it. Ms. Patricia rests an arm around my shoulders as she guides me to the main office cabin, a rickety wooden structure that wouldn't hesitate to give a million splinters to anyone who brushes against a wall. I love it.

"It's so good to see you again," Ms. Patricia says, her hand tightening against my arm. "How have you been?"

I think of my girlfriend—my *ex*-girlfriend—plastered all over social media, my name probably being reprinted on my birth certificate as "the dumb idiot who used to think Ally would love her forever even after she became *the* Allyson Hendricks" as we speak. "It's going so super awesome, actually."

"Convincing," Ms. Patricia says wryly, but she doesn't pry further.

I nudge her shoulder with mine. "How's camp doing?"

"So super awesome, actually," she says, raising her voice an octave to match mine, and I roll my eyes at her.

She pulls open the door of the main office, and the splintering exterior gives way to the cozy inside: hand-knitted throw blankets, a fraying couch with cushions so worn they threaten to swallow any sitter whole, and a hot water station that has soaked the whole room with the smell of hot chocolate. An ancient desk wobbles by the door, the ramshackle home to an even more ancient desktop computer.

"Sign in when the spinny wheel stops turning," Ms. Patricia says, releasing my shoulder to gesture at the frozen computer screen. I slump in front of it, waiting for the form to load. Once it does, I set about checking a long series of boxes chronicling my past experience with the camp and my goals for the summer. I'm here in part—in large part, while I'm being honest—to prove to my dad that majoring in education is a good move. My school's college admissions counselor made the entire junior class draft our college essays during finals week, winning her the dubious honor of making the least popular decision in education history. Ever since my dad read it, he's been fretting aloud about how "restrictive" an education major would be for me.

It only leads to one career path, he's told me more than once in the ten-day stretch between the day my essay draft was due and this morning, when he squeezed it in one last time over breakfast. *A pretty underpaid and underappreciated one at that.*

He's not wrong, though I'm pretty sure most of his fretting is fueled by resentment toward my mom, who as far as we know still teaches fourth grade. But if I can spend this summer proving that I'm good at this, that I can connect with kids and make a difference in their lives after two short months together, maybe the whole majoring-in-education operation will seem more viable to him.

There's no box for that on the form, though, so I check "other" and move on.

As I do, the rickety front door slams open, and a pale, freckled boy with floppy brown hair stretches out his hands to greet Broccoli, who scampers across the floor, tail wagging so hard his whole butt shakes with it.

"This is Fitz," Ms. Patricia says. "And Ben," she adds as Fitz is followed by a boy wearing a loose floral T-shirt and sharp gold eyeliner that glows against his dark skin.

She points back to me. "This is Ivy. Just waiting on one more. You'll meet the other two at the campfire."

"You said the orientation was mandatory," Ben protests. "You also said snacks," he adds, making a show of peering around the room.

"That's my bad." Fitz crosses the room to flop onto the couch. It swallows him whole. "I was in here earlier. There, uh, was once a bowl of chips and some guac."

"I wonder what happened," Ben says as he takes a seat next to Fitz, a wry grin spreading across his face. "A mystery to join the Case of the Last Cinnamon Roll."

I bite my lip, watching the easy way they tease each other. When Dad insisted I stay home with the family as long as possible, I didn't think I'd miss out on much, given that the schedule Ms. Patricia emailed only offered an "optional s'mores bonding night and continental breakfast" for early arrival counselors.

I rack my brain for a joke—just one! Even a feeble one would do!—to contribute to the group's gentle ribbing, but my single brain cell is busy singing the same commercial jingle that's been stuck there all morning. Great. I'm not even dating Ally anymore, but I'm still stuck playing "who's that quiet girl over there?"

A girl with long auburn hair tied in a loose bun, who Ms. P introduces as Celia, makes her way into the main office, and Ms. Patricia gestures for the rest of us to sit down. I claim the armchair next to Celia, who gives me a small smile that instantly puts me more at ease. In the moment of silence that follows, I take a deep breath. The smell of pine and fresh air drifting from the open window eases my stuttering heartbeat. The rest of them might be settling into an easy camaraderie, but I only missed one night. There's the whole summer left to unfurl. I'll find my place here.

Hopefully.

"First on the agenda," Ms. Patricia says. "Introductions. Talk to the person next to you for one minute. This is for bonding, and not at all because I forgot the binder in my room."

With that, she dashes out of the door. Next to me, Celia snorts.

"I love her. I'm Celia Martinez," she adds. "I think our groups are sharing a cabin."

We're each assigned a core group of five campers and partnered with one counselor to share a cabin and another to form day groups. I'm grateful Celia, with her broad smile and stern eyes, will be my ally for enforcing bedtime.

"Do you know when dinner is?" I ask as my stomach rumbles.

Celia shakes her head. "I flew in from New York last night, and I have no idea what time it is."

"From New York?" I gape at her. "To *here*? Why?"

I didn't think anyone but me would ever love this place enough to think it's worth a cross-country red-eye flight.

"Ms. Patricia said I could lead the ballet classes, and that's really my thing," Celia says. Ballet isn't usually the dance focus, given that we're a musical theater camp, but Ms. P is a firm believer in both variety in training and empowering her counselors to pursue their interests. "Plus, this place smells way better than the city does in the summer. The main thing is that if I go to college, I want to come out here. So this is really a practice run. For my parents."

I laugh along with her. She asks what brought me here, but

before I can launch into my whole life story, Ms. Patricia comes rushing back, her arms wrapped around a thick blue binder.

"Okay, first things first," she says, flipping to the first page in the binder. "Safety protocols."

As she launches into fire drills, I stare, disheartened, at the unbelievably thick stack of papers left to get through. The next item on the emailed agenda for the day is Campfire, with Cabin Setup followed by Mandatory Icebreakers (with S'mores) tomorrow, and I've been daydreaming about the mandatory marshmallows all morning. If I'm being honest, I'm also antsy for a moment alone so I can finally read the stupid press release Ally's publicist put out about me. About us. And how we are no longer an *us*. An infinite scroll of fan reactions is one thing, but I want to know what she said. Or at least what her representatives said.

Across from me, Fitz is melting off the couch in boredom as we move from fires to earthquakes to lockdowns, and Ms. Patricia finally turns the page to counselor cabin assignments. I sit up straighter in my seat as she hands me a list naming my day group: the ten tweens I'll be responsible for all summer. I'll be the one to shepherd them to their activities, hang out with them during free play, and help them through the rare sad moment at camp. I've been practicing my "how to recover from homesickness" speech in the mirror. Though based on my own camp memories, I'm not expecting any problems past the first day. Acorn Hill is way too much fun to spend a second worrying about missing home.

The rest of the binder takes an eternity to get through. Ms. P walks us through first aid principles, the camp map, handling allergies 101, and the camp calendar before finally snapping the Binder of Eternal Boredom shut. A silent sigh of relief passes over all the counselors.

"Oh, one more thing," Ms. Patricia says, and I deflate as she sets the binder onto the coffee table. "I'll be holding interviews this week to find the director for the end-of-summer musical. Sign up here if you're interested. It comes with lots of extra work and absolutely no extra money."

She pulls a sheet of lined paper out of the binder and lays it on the coffee table. I scoot toward it, teetering on the edge of the armchair. I'm a solidly mediocre singer, and I'm definitely not god's gift to acting, so I spent most of my summers in the end-of-camp musical ensemble, with the exception of one year when Ms. P took pity on me and gave me a speaking role. Directing, though, sounds right up my alley, in that I love being in charge. And being in charge of *this* could be the perfect way to leave my creative mark on this camp that shaped so much of my childhood.

I don't hesitate. As soon as Ms. Patricia releases us, I dash out of my seat and make to snatch the pen and add my name. It's a mercifully short list—only one of the returning counselors has signed up, via illegible scrawl. I scribble my name in the second slot, crossing my fingers around the pen as I do.

BY THE TIME I'M DONE FILLING OUT ALL THE ONBOARD-ing forms and changing into a warmer outfit, the sun has set and the heat of the day has evaporated into a mountain-cooled night. I hunch my shoulders in my gray hoodie and make my way down the grassy slope to the firepit, where the other counselors are already dipping marshmallow-tipped sticks into the flames. I grab a stick and a marshmallow as I scan the huddle for a place to sit.

There's only one empty spot, so I'm swinging my leg over the log in what I'm sure is an extremely graceful move when I catch sight of the girl across the fire.

She's turned to face Fitz as he talks about his audition for his high school's spring production of *Bye Bye Birdie*. The firelight lands gently in the angles of her face, lighting her eyes behind her glasses, and for a moment the thought enters my head, unbidden: *she's so beautiful.* It feels ridiculous, a thought like that nipping at the heels of Ally. My heart is still so broken, yearning for a second chance at what I had with her. Yet here I am, momentarily helpless as I lean toward this girl, eyes brightened by firelight.

But then she laughs, and the thought dissolves as the sound washes over me, startling in its familiarity. I reel back, almost falling off the log. Because there's no way, absolutely no way, that I can actually be hearing this voice for the first time since sixth grade, when the owner of said voice was busy saying *I never want to be your friend again.*

She meant it, too. I haven't seen her since.

But it is. There *she* is. That same voice. The same short dark hair, the tips now dyed teal. The same round blue glasses that slip down her crooked nose every time she wrinkles it, which she always does when she laughs.

Rynn Walsh.

Our eyes meet, but she doesn't recognize me. Not right away. She lifts her hand in a half wave, lips parted, and I can tell she's about to introduce herself. And then her eyes flash with recognition, with shock, with something else I can't quite make out in the depth of her murky brown irises.

"Ivy?" Her voice, still familiar even after five years of silence, warbles in a way I recognize. It's the same way she sounded when we had a math pop quiz. The thought makes me bristle. I hate how well I know her, in that well-worn way that grows out of childhood. But now it's just a reminder that I have no idea who she is anymore.

"Hi, Rynn," I say, because what else is a person supposed to say to their childhood best friend turned biggest platonic heartbreak turned complete stranger turned . . . coworker? "Are you . . . a counselor this year? At *my* summer camp?" The last part slips out without me entirely meaning for it to, and the shock on her face curdles.

"Yours?"

"I spent every summer of our childhood here," I remind her.

"I've been a counselor here for years," she says, shifting her weight on the log. "Since I was a CIT."

I indulge in some mental math, knowing even before I start counting that the result is going to hurt my feelings. The CIT program at Acorn Hill was for thirteen-year-olds, which means . . .

"You started coming here a *year* after you . . ." I can't bring myself to say *dumped me.* It was a million years ago. I'm not still smarting over how she ended our friendship. Given that we were twelve, it was only fair that it involved a bit of drama. But the shock of seeing her has scrambled my thoughts. "After we . . . After I moved away?"

She knots her fingers together and lets out the world's most forced laugh. "Ivy and I went to middle school together," she says, gesturing toward me as she looks around at the rest of the group.

I'm frozen in place on my log, the iciness of this shock tethering me to the splintering seat. Rynn? Here? *How?* She meets my eyes, a smile reaching hers, as she suddenly leans toward me. The firelight glows in the dips and curves of her face, and for a moment I find myself drawn to her, leaning in across the fire as well.

But then she blows out the little fire that has started where I dipped my marshmallow too long into the flames and settles back on her seat. I flush, leaning back as though the fire has burned me.

"Well, welcome to the party," Fitz says, beaming at me. "We were just going around and sharing our life stories. I'm almost done, and then it's your turn."

Panic strikes, and my heart feels like it's pumping acid through my chest as Fitz finishes telling us about his aspirations to be an actor, though his parents are insisting he go for a basketball scholarship at his state school. I'm trying to make friends, not out myself as the most dumped person here. Or possibly anywhere. Lots of people get dumped, but how many people get their own sad-sack dumpee hashtag?

Fitz's story must be over because he turns to me expectantly.

"What's your deal?" he asks as he crushes a mostly burnt marshmallow between two thick, gluteny graham crackers.

"I . . ." My brain short-circuits. What could I possibly tell them about myself? *Well, I've been dumped by everyone who's ever been important to me, including my first girlfriend and my mom and sort of my dad if you count not really liking me as a proper dumping, and on top of that, the entire* Telephone Hour *fandom, which comprises of almost a million people, is rejoicing in the most recent dumping experience and celebrating the occasion by posting BecAlly edits all over every corner of the internet! Thanks for asking!* "I came to this camp as a kid."

It's a lame answer. I can tell from the second it takes everyone to realize I have nothing more to offer. Great. Now I look like the resident Standoffish Ass Who's Too Good to Share. But I can hardly tell them that I am in fact not good enough to share, so I settle for spearing a marshmallow onto the end of my roasting stick and popping it directly into the flames, sparks spitting at me as I lean closer to do so.

"Anything else?"

I look up to face Rynn, who's sitting across the firepit from me. The flickering orange light sharpens the angles of her face. I can't tell if she's trying to help or if she's baiting me. Or if she's just as shocked as I am.

"I could trot out some embarrassing childhood stories, but I'm not sure the present company wants that." I try to keep my tone light, like I'm talking to an old friend, but the words drip heavy from my mouth.

"Fire away." Rynn grins as she leans back, her pale pink sundress rustling around her knees. A taunt. At least it seems that way. I have no idea how to read her anymore.

"One time I made a joke so funny that Rynn peed her pants laughing on a school camping trip, and had to be issued a new sleeping bag," I say, grinning at the memory.

She laughs along with the others. "You're not *that* funny. I was too afraid to go in the woods!"

"I remember a lot of 'No! Stop! My abs hurt!' happening."

"It doesn't beat the time you laughed so hard, you spat milk all over our third-grade teacher in the cafeteria," Rynn says. The firelight hardens the angles of her pale face.

I force a brittle laugh, my annoyance simmering just underneath. I still can't believe she's here. After so many years. Holding court at *my* summer camp. My one safe haven during my middle school years of suffering.

Well, one of two havens. The other being Rynn's childhood bedroom. A cozy space with a window reading nook lined with pillows, a full wall of crammed-to-the-brim bookshelves, and a corner dedicated to a bed, toy bin, and treat jar for her dog.

"You named your dog Cat," I reminded her.

"You named your dog Peanut Butter," she protests.

My heart goes squishy as I remember Peanut Butter. He was the best boy—an ancient golden retriever we adopted from a local shelter to fill his last years with good food and easy hikes and soft touches against his fur. There's no feeling more peaceful in the world than the weight of Peanut Butter's head as he fell asleep on your thigh.

"Cat is way more embarrassing," Ben confirms, and I crow with delight.

As if to celebrate my victory, my marshmallow goes from burnt to actively on fire. A flare goes up in the fire, and I scream, jumping back, but seeing as I'm still clutching the roasting stick in my panicked fingers, the flaming marshmallow follows me. Yelping, I drop it, and my would-be s'more lands safely back in the pit.

Next to me, Fitz and Ben have dissolved in laughter. Rynn falls behind Celia as she howls.

"Who's more embarrassing now, Ben?" Rynn chokes out.

In answer, Ben mimics my flight backward and accidentally trips over a log, sending us all in an uproar again.

"Guess the answer has to be you, buddy," Fitz says, leaning over to offer Ben a hand and pulling him to his feet.

Ben dusts off his pants, which are covered in dirt. "You're all traitors. I thought we were ganging up on these two."

"Yeah, until you presented us with a better option," Celia says, grinning.

"I'm quitting," Ben says, shaking his head as he retakes his seat on the log by Fitz.

I grab a new marshmallow and roasting stick, and Fitz stands, throwing his hands out to call our attention.

"As the squad's self-appointed fire captain, I need to alert you all that Ms. Ivy Raines is about to attempt a s'more. Please maintain at least six feet of distance."

Celia and Rynn make a big show of lifting their log and moving it back. I bite back the smile tugging at the corners of my lips as I pull my roasting stick back from the flames and sandwich the marshmallow between two slabs of chocolate. Fitz bursts into applause.

"Counselors of Acorn Hill, I'm thrilled to share that the danger has passed. Please resume your normal activities," he intones. "And with that, Ben, I believe it was your turn to tell us your life story."

Ben tells us about his shirt (it turns out the florals are his own design, dyed from wildflowers collected around his neighborhood), how he wants to be a singer, and the ex-boyfriend he left back home. I consider jumping on his breakup bandwagon, until he tells us the breakup story.

"Breaking up with him was for sure one of the hardest things I've ever had to do," Ben says. He stares into the fire, his elbows digging into his knees, and Fitz's hand hovers in the air between them for a moment before he pats Ben on the shoulder. "He took it so hard. Like, I actually broke his heart. I'm still not sure how anyone moves on from that."

"I'm so sorry," Celia says, the firelight glowing against her warm brown skin as she leans forward to pat his knee. "It sounds like you did the right thing."

The rest of the group hums in agreement, and I retreat into my little shell of embarrassment. Given how gleefully Rynn has already made fun of me today, I can't hand her more ammunition. I certainly don't want everyone to join me in wondering what I did to prompt Ally to dump me. Best to keep the past in the past, where it belongs. I settle cross-legged on my log, biting into my chocolate s'more, and watch the campfire spit sparks at the stars.

Geek TV | Top Five Reasons I'm a Proud #TeleFan

By Cassie Parker

1. I'm a space nerd and the landscapes are breathtaking. Who else can't wait to finally see the Silent Planet?!

2. I always need more rogue space smugglers in my life.

3. I cry every time the Telephone Hour strikes and my precious band of smuggler rebels finally gets to call Earth. Every. Single. Time.

4. Artis and Milo's friendship is everything!!!

5. Whenever Artis gets to call her earthbound girlfriend, Hemilia, I legit sob. #TEAMBECALLYFOREVER

I STILL HAVEN'T READ THE PRESS RELEASE. MY PHONE is steaming in my pocket, begging me to reach for it. I couldn't bring myself to open it last night, not after the shock of seeing Rynn again. I'm reeling enough already.

Which is not a great state to be in when I'm also balanced on the edge of a dresser, straining to reach the ceiling in a desperate attempt to tape up the last corner of the Welcome to Camp banner I made for my cabin. This is where five of the campers in my day group will share bunk beds and secrets and the best summers of their young lives, alongside the five campers from Celia's group. Celia volunteered to help set up the dance studio, so I'm taking over cabin decor.

I finally get the piece of tape to stick to the wall, and I hop off the dresser to survey my handiwork. I got the kids mini teddy bears, one propped up on each bare bunk bed mattress. My banner, which I've now noticed is crooked, drapes across the center of the room. I'm contemplating taking my life into my hands and climbing onto the dresser again to fix it when the cabin door bangs open.

I spin on my heel, my sneaker soles grinding up dust. On the threshold, Rynn is shrinking from the slamming sound the door made when she opened it. It's not technically her fault—the door only has one setting, and that setting is slam. But it's such a microcosm of how I feel right now: caught completely off guard, Rynn slamming back into my life after so many years of silence.

That yearslong silence continues for thirty seconds that feel just as long.

"I can't believe you're here," she says quietly. Her fingers run down her arm to the fraying cuffs of her baggy sweatshirt.

I'm not sure how to respond, so I don't right away. I lean against the dresser, taking in her face. It's changed so much since I last saw it—obviously it has, but every time I've thought of Rynn, I've pictured her gangly twelve-year-old limbs and crooked pre-braces smile. Even the freckles constellating around her nose have faded. Her eyes are the only thing that look the same, but meeting them is charged in a whole new way now. They've become another reminder that I have no idea how to read the girl within them anymore.

"I can't believe you're here," I repeat.

She gives a small laugh, tugging her sleeves over her hands as she tucks them across her chest. "This is so weird. I mean, I never thought I'd see you here."

I bristle against the thought. Given how our last conversation went, it's hard not to hear *I never wanted to see you here* hiding behind her words.

"I guess I came to . . . break the ice," Rynn says. "Last night felt weird. I was so surprised to see you, I didn't know how to be."

"Me neither," I admit. I've been cringing at the memory of everything I said last night all morning. I didn't mean to come off like I was antagonizing her. I just have no idea how to actually connect with her anymore. It doesn't help that I'm still reeling from Ally dumping me—the last thing I needed was this living, breathing reminder of my first platonic dumping experience.

"Are you . . . excited for the campers to come tomorrow?" Rynn asks. She glances around the cabin. "Your banner is crooked."

I stiffen. This is how she wants to break the ice? With immediate criticism? "I was just about to fix it."

Her cheeks flush, and it's finally something in this new Rynn that I recognize. Her face has always betrayed her emotions. "Shit, sorry, I meant— Can I help you fix it?"

"Sure." I shift my weight so I can hop back onto the dresser. "Thanks."

Another heavy silence falls, and I shudder under the weight of its awkwardness. This is a girl I used to spill all my secrets to. We used to fall asleep next to each other in matching sleeping bags on Saturday nights. Now I can't think of a single thing to say to her.

"Do you know what they're doing for the camp musical this year?" I ask as she holds down the other end of the banner so I can lift mine. It's embarrassingly small-talky as far as questions go, but anything is better than this palpable silence.

"No idea," Rynn says. "I've asked Ms. P to tell me a million times, but she won't. You'd think she would, given that I'm going to direct it."

She smiles at me conspiratorially, as if she's trying to turn this into a fun bonding moment where we all have a laugh about how annoying Ms. P can be. But first of all, I'm never one to complain about Ms. P. Not after everything she did for me when I was a kid.

And second?

"How do you know you're directing it?" I ask. My tone is hard, and all the awkwardness that Rynn thought she was diffusing comes back to throttle the air between us. "I mean, I'm going for the job, too."

"What?" Rynn's fingers tighten on the end of the banner. "But I've been a counselor here since I was old enough to be. Ms. P started the job so I could . . . I mean—"

"I was a camper here before you even knew this place existed," I point out. If she's going to use seniority to snatch the job from me, she'll have to do better than *I got here first.* "There are still the interviews. You can't just automatically claim the job."

Rynn blinks fast, her eyelashes fluttering behind her glasses. The morning sunlight catches in their lenses. "I just thought . . . I've been planning around doing it. Directing, I mean. It's really important to me."

I stare at her. Is she seriously suggesting I should back out of the interviews so she can just . . . have it?

"It's important to me, too," I say simply. That feels like the understatement of the year. *Directing the musical is all I have going for me right now* feels like a more accurate one. After Ally, I'm in desperate need of something that's just *mine.* Something I can control, shape how I want—something that can define the mark I leave on this camp, other than the weirdo disaster I've been so far in my first day here. I'm not about to cede that to Rynn "I deserve it automatically because I weirdly took over your summer camp and now think that gives me seniority claims" Walsh.

"Well." Rynn swallows and stretches her lips into a wobbly

smile. It's so forced, it looks copy-pasted on. "I guess we'll just have to compete for it."

"I guess so."

And with that, I trip backward and tumble off the dresser.

Rynn screeches and lunges forward in time to break my fall. We both crash to the ground, and I'm saved from any broken bones. Though I might've taken a shattered ankle over the purple bruise that's currently flowering over my ego. For a moment we're trapped in a tangle of limbs.

"Thanks," I say, my tone as sharp as I can make it without sounding completely ungrateful.

"This sucks," Rynn says.

I nod, but I don't know how to make it unsuck, so I let the silence settle back over us.

Rynn winces as she stretches her ankle, rolling it under her. "Look. Maybe us being friends again isn't going to happen."

The thought hardens a lump in my throat, but I know she's right. Things were awkward enough before we found out that we've pitted ourselves against each other for this job that apparently means so much to both of us.

"I guess we just have to agree to be professionals," Rynn finishes, sticking out her hand.

I sigh. I want a lot of things right now. Getting Allyson back is at the top of the list, even though I know that's never going to happen, followed closely by the director job. I want to finish setting up my cabin so my campers will love their summer home away from home when they get in tomorrow morning. I want there to be a good gluten-free vegetarian meatball option to go with tonight's spaghetti dinner.

Absolutely nowhere on my list of yearnings is to have a stilted professional relationship with my ex–best friend.

"Professionals," I say, so bitingly I accidentally chomp on my inner cheek.

She shakes on it, but when our eyes meet, both of our gazes are steely.

"NO."

"No way."

We say it at the same time, on instinct, and even though I obviously agree with her, I resent it.

"We have to do trust falls," Ms. P insists, her bobbed brown hair wobbling as she shakes her head. "It's a camp staple."

The thought of catching Rynn, of letting her fall into my arms, after how entitled she was this morning when she was coming after my one last hope and dream, makes my skin crawl. I try to laugh it off. "I can't trust the competition."

"Can't I catch Celia? Or Ben?" Rynn asks. "Or Fitz? Or myself?"

"Or a clue?" I mutter.

The other counselors are sharing confused looks, and even the pine trees surrounding our little clearing feel judgy. I can't say I blame them. I've been shoved right back into my sixth-grade headspace in that way only encounters with long-ago frenemies can do. I might be standing in this clearing as a full fifteen-year-old girl among the tall grass and blossomed yellow wildflowers, but my brain has relodged itself into that gangly twelve-year-old kid full of too much angst and not enough sense.

An awkward silence descends, punctuated by the staccato work of a nearby woodpecker. I stare Rynn down, not blinking away from her brown eyes for even a moment, painfully aware of how idiotic I'm being. Still, I won't be the first to give in.

"Fine," Ms. P says at last, throwing her hands up. "Celia, Ivy, you be partners."

Rynn flounces over to Fitz, and I spin on my heel toward Celia.

"Thanks," I say awkwardly. With Rynn safely out of sight, I feel my brain turn fifteen again and internally cringe at how Celia must see me now. The only thing she knows about me is that I refuse to play nice with others.

"No worries," she says. "You and Rynn seem to have . . . history."

"A nice way of putting it," I say with a wry laugh.

Now that we've all been placed in satisfactory pairs, we arrange ourselves in a circle in the middle of the clearing. It's only a ten-minute walk from camp, but the bends in the path through the thick trees have blocked our view of the cabins, giving the pleasant feeling of standing in the middle of nowhere.

Ms. Patricia stands in the middle of the circle, her whistle bouncing against the red Camp Acorn Hill lettering on her sweatshirt. "On my mark, one of you falls into the other. No communication ahead of time for which one of you will be falling and which will be catching."

"Wait, what?" Celia and I both ask at the same time, but Ms. P gives a puff of her whistle. We both move to catch each other, then giggle when we crash into each other instead.

"This exercise is about forming a deeper bond," Ms. P says. "I know none of you are bold enough to drop each other while I'm watching—"

"I wouldn't be so sure," Rynn shouts from across the clearing.

"Interrupting is rude," I yell back at her.

Ms. P smoothly ignores us both. "—so we're going to dig deeper. On my whistle."

This time, Celia and I both fall. Rynn, however, manages to neatly catch Fitz. They do a whole spinning-and-cheering routine, and Celia and I exchange good-humored eye rolls.

"One more time," calls Ms. P, before blowing her whistle again.

I start to fall, but pivot to catch Celia in time, her back thudding against my forearms. It's our turn to cheer, and we high-five, our palms slapping together loudly enough to outdo the woodpecker. Next to us, Fitz and Ben have both landed hard against the grass, stirring up a nearby patch of dandelions in the process.

"Make a wish," Fitz shrieks as the freed dandelion puffs catch on the breeze and float past us.

A hush falls again. I screw my eyes shut and wish for the musical director job, for Rynn to just go ahead and leave me alone, and for none of the counselors to check their social media platform of choice before the discourse about me and Ally has died down. After my all-too-public spat with Rynn, the last thing I need is for everyone to find out I'm a freshly dumped Hollywood romance castoff.

When I open my eyes, all the dandelion pappi have disappeared into the grass, and Ms. P is calling us to dinner.

THE SUN SET AGES AGO, AND THE UNSEASONABLY cool day has transformed into a chilly night. I zip my hoodie to the top as I make my way from the dining hall cabin (where there were absolutely no gluten-free vegetarian meatball options to go with the spaghetti dinner—the two circles in my Venn diagram of hellish dietary restrictions refused to overlap yet again) to the firepit, which is already crackling in anticipation of mandatory s'mores.

I fiddle with the edges of my PopSocket, which I only got because I found one that looks just like Nugget, as I stare at the blinking cursor in my notes app. Since lunch I've been trying to turn off the part of my brain that's shouting *JUST TEXT HER* over and over and over again.

I want to *so badly*. Hearing from her would be like taking an emotional painkiller. An ibuprofen straight to the heart. Enough to tide me over for a few hours before the dull ache would inevitably work its way back into my system.

Safe in the darkness of the new moon night, the other counselors already bouncing ahead of me toward the promise of marshmallows and chocolate, I pause and take a seat under a particularly thick-trunked tree. Its roots rise in bumps and ridges, sprawling hugely at its base, and I settle in their protective embrace. Above me, the sky is littered with stars. I haven't seen this many in a long time—there's too much light pollution in San Francisco—but they look just like I remember them.

I had this teacher when I was a freshman, Ms. Avril, who was just out of her teacher prep program and prone to oversharing in an attempt to bond with us. It worked: I was completely obsessed with her. She talked endlessly about her new puppy and her newer boyfriend, and the day after she broke up with him was the most drama-filled day of my early teen years.

Never cry when someone is dumping you, guys, she'd said from behind wide-rimmed sunglasses that undoubtedly covered puffy eyes. *Just say "okay" like you're so unbothered. Save the tears for when they leave.*

To thirteen-year-old me, those were just about the wisest words I'd ever heard. So when I found myself bawling in front of Ally after she said the fateful words, I felt like such an idiot.

Why? What happened? It was all I could keep asking.

Nothing happened, she'd assured me. *We just have such different lives now. We don't fit anymore.*

I ugly-sobbed right there in front of her, snot dribbling down my face. I couldn't help myself. She'd been making me feel so much smaller than her for months leading up to it, and at last she was saying it out loud: she didn't think I was enough for her anymore. I was just a footnote in the "early life" section of her Wikipedia page. I didn't belong with her now that she was a huge national deal and I was just a quiet high school kid with small-town aspirations of becoming a teacher. My face burns now as I remember what I must've looked like, sobbing in front of her like that. What a great last image of me I created for her.

I haven't cried since. I'm not interested in wallowing through the stages of grieving a relationship. I don't want to go *through* this. I want *this* to simply go away. Getting back together would be the perfect, instant balm to make all the hurt disappear. As if none of this ever happened. If that's not possible, then I'd like to skip right to the acceptance stage. And for that, I need closure.

I pull up my notes app and go back to what's been my favorite Allyson-related hobby these days: staring at that damn cursor. With a deep breath and a lungful of cool night air to spur me forward, I start typing.

Hey!

And with that, I start backspacing. Too glib.

Hi Ally.

Too familiar?

Allyson—

Way too formal. I go back to *Hi Ally.* We might have broken up, but we'll always be familiar. Like Rynn's voice, rushing back to me as soon as I heard it again all these years later. When you've known someone all the way, to their marrow, no amount of time and space can dislodge them.

Hi Ally it is.

The way we left things feels rough. I'm not asking to get back together, and I don't think either of us is ready to be friends right now, but OH MY GOD CAN WE JUST TALK IT OUT AND

MAYBE EVERYTHING WILL BE OKAY AND AS IT WAS AND YOU WILL LOVE ME AGAIN??????

It all comes pouring out in a flash of thumbs. My chest tightens and my throat thickens, and I swallow hard as I hit the backspace key 253 times. My eyes are bone dry, and I swipe at them as I get up. I guess now isn't quite the time to draft this text. Ignoring the notifications pouring in on my family group chat, I switch to my web browser. If I can't text her, maybe now, with the stars to watch over me and the roots to keep me safe, is the time to finally read that press release.

Sources close to the couple means Juliana, Ally's publicist. Which makes the phrase *the couple* a bit of a stretch. She has Ally's interests in mind, not mine.

The worst part is, I like Juliana. She was always nice to me when seeing my name in the tabloids freaked me out, and she helped shield us from the worst of the internet's fascination with us as a couple. It was easy to forget that she was only really a part of Team Ally when I was on Team Ally, too.

That's why she's claiming that *the split was mutual, and Ally remains close friends with her former girlfriend even though their romance has run its course.* The corner of the *Telephone Hour* fandom that was obsessed with our relationship loved it in part because they loved cooing about how *down-to-earth* Ally must be to still date her nobody high school girlfriend after becoming so famous. They would hardly love to hear how unceremoniously Ally dumped said high school nobody once she didn't need me anymore.

I tip my neck back to lean against the tree, the ridges of the bark digging into the back of my head. My eyes close, and as per usual when I do that lately, I'm flooded with the memory of Ally's eyes the afternoon she broke up with me. They were full of sun—the weather had no idea what was happening to me that day, and I was dumped in the thick of late-spring morning romance, alive with birdsong and cherry blossom showers. The sun made them gorgeous, bringing out their deep blue color, but that isn't what haunts me. It's how *done* she was.

I'd trade anything for the memory of grief in her eyes, even just a hint of sadness. Hell, I'd take anger, even. Any trace of an emotion deeper than the awkward discomfort that comes with telling someone something they don't want to hear.

"I'll always love you" were the words she said. "I just don't think this relationship works anymore. We're holding each other back."

Her eyes said, *I just don't give a shit anymore.* They dismissed our entire relationship. As if none of it ever mattered to her.

Because what she really meant was *"You're* holding *me* back." She'd spent the last several months of our relationship making that clear. The only person more vocal than my dad about his worries that I have my heart too set on teaching was Ally. She must've introduced me to a thousand industry people with heaping praise about how great my writing is. She told me a million times that she thought I could aspire to *more.* So that we could be *on the same level.*

The worst part about that comment is I didn't even have enough steel in my spine to point out how demeaning it was. My heart had lashed out right away. *Oh, so right now I'm beneath you?* But my lips stayed tightly pressed together.

I get why Juliana isn't putting that in the press release.

The feathery ruffle of a bird taking flight rustles the branches above me, and I look up to let the starlight wash over my face. I wish I was the kind of person who could look back on all that and think definitively, *Well, I'm better off without her.* But I'd have to overlook all the sweet times we shared. We had a baking tradition, where every month we'd write each other a love letter and bake something new. A way of staying connected in spite of the distance. It started off easy enough—cookies and brownies and cupcakes that'd arrive with the frosting smudged. But the mandate of *new* soon brought us to frantically googling "how to ship tiramisu" and laughing over FaceTime as we struggled with perfecting a reasonably edible gluten-free bread.

Not to mention our love story. Half the fandom was obsessed with our story—how could I not be? Meeting in middle school, loving each other through our awkward pubescent years, and learning to turn that into something real, something that felt so solid beneath me. Surviving the odds of youth, distance, fame. Until, suddenly, we weren't.

How could I not want that back?

How could I not yearn for her to see me again as someone who could build her up instead of bringing her down?

I don't realize tears have slipped from my eyes until Broccoli leaves his post sniffing for marshmallows by the campfire to come snuffling over to me. He thumps his entire body to the ground in one fell swoop, nosing at my pockets. I scratch him behind the ears, letting my fingers tangle into his mass of golden fur, and try to breathe.

3

AllysonHendricks [2 days ago]: life lately . . .

LilyRoseFrazier: omg is that the silent planet!!!!!!! Tuesday cannot come soon enough!!!!!!!

NiallHartley: thank you so much for letting us into your grieving process. breakups are so hard and you're helping so many people. xoxo sending love and strength

StephanieWilliams: love the behind-the-scenes peeks but who else was hoping for a #BecAlly relationship reveal . . .

EllisReynolds: her private life is just that—private!

StephanieWilliams: she's a celebrity and has made a lot of her dating life public in the past . . . we're allowed to speculate if we want!!

ElodieDonovan: she and her ex JUST broke up . . . there's no way they're together (yet)

StephanieWilliams: we all know why they broke up though . . .

LucyGiles: FACTS

RosieFord: sending love Allyson! we TeleFans are behind you!

—✿—

I SPENT THE LAST MONTH OF SCHOOL READING teacher books in preparation for today. Some of them were mostly boring, some of them were amazing—I may have sent a copy of one to my school's principal with a note to see the passage on doing away with grades. Most of them had chapters on the importance of the first days of school. Establishing routines, forming relationships, setting the community culture. It's basically the most important time of the school year—or summer break, in this case.

I thought I was ready.

Now, standing among the chaos of an overflooded lot full of triple-parked cars, a zillion duffel bags smacking passersby in the face as unwitting campers turn to give their parents goodbye hugs, and counselors shouting directions and cabin assignments, I know the truth: I. Am. Not. Ready. No amount of reading could ever have prepared me for this moment, for the reality of parents handing their precious children off to me, of the tweens I'm directly responsible for looking at me expectantly.

Overwhelmed is an understatement.

"I'm Twyla Pepperson," a girl with an adorable smattering of freckles and brunette curls knotted into a thick braid says as she bounces up to me.

I check my clipboard, the only thing anchoring me to my tenuous authority right now. "Hi, Twyla, it's so nice to meet you."

"Haven't we met before?" she asks, tipping her head at me.

I shake my head.

"You weren't a counselor or something last year?" she asks. "You look so familiar."

"I wasn't last year, but this year you're in my group," I tell her, and she shrugs. "Our day group is gathering over by the basketball hoop with Counselor Fitz, and then I'll lead you all to the cabins once everyone is checked in."

"Thanks." She grins, flashing blue-wire braces, before scurrying off to join Wally Timur, Josie Winston, and Arlo Rocky, the three other kids in my group who have already checked in. They've gathered around Fitz, who's letting them beat him at basketball. I smile as I watch him, thanking Ms. P and the universe that I'm sharing a cabin with Celia and a day group with Fitz and, most important, neither with Rynn. Celia's sharing her day group with Ben, and Rynn gets her own day group. Ms. P claims it's because she has enough experience that she can handle a group on her own, a move made necessary by camp budget cuts, but I suspect it's because no one would want to work with her.

Celia weaves her way through the crowd, almost tripping over a stray backpack as she reaches me. "Can you believe this?"

"No," I answer honestly, speaking too loud so she can hear me over the brouhaha of overlapping conversations around us. There's no way to bluff my way through how out of my depth I feel. "This is absolutely bananas."

The coolness we enjoyed yesterday has evaporated under the beating sun, and even though it's still midmorning, I've already ditched my breezy summer flannel in favor of a thick-strapped tank top and jean shorts. I'm still sweating way too much for my campers to think I'm cool.

"I don't know how Rynn is doing it," she says, glancing over her shoulder at the middle of the parking lot, where Rynn is somehow checking in campers, assuaging tearful parents, and applying the first Band-Aid of the summer to a freshly skinned knee all at the same time.

"She's got more experience is all," I say, shrugging to underplay how impressed I am. "We'll be at her level in no time."

If I'm going to convince my dad (and, if we're being honest here, myself) that teaching is a good idea, I can't lose the title of Best Counselor of the Summer to *Rynn*. Bad enough that I've spent the past four years playing second fiddle to *The Ally Show: A Nonstop Success Story*. I'm tired of being bested.

Celia starts to answer, but is cut off by Sammy Baxter and Ella Beare, two more names I get to check off my day group list.

"My group is gathered by the hoops," I tell them before turning back to Celia. "Seriously, I'm sure she was just as lost as we are her first year."

"My kids are adorable," Celia says.

I glance at my own group of tweens. Twyla is eagerly chatting

41

at Emma Tuxall, but the rest are awkwardly milling around, working hard at not making eye contact. "They really are."

"I already have a matchmaking plan hatching," Celia adds with a wink. "Two of my campers are from the same school, and one of them turned so beet red when she saw he's in her group that he must be her crush."

I feel my cheeks turning as beet red as Celia's camper's. Ever since everyone and their online aunt started gossiping about my breakup, I've started grating against the way people talk about romance. Tween crushes are supposed to be fun, and making a big deal out of them makes me prickle awkwardly, like a reminder of all those comments that inevitably accumulated under all of Ally's posts, cooing about how we were their favorite couple.

Before I can argue—or even decide if I'm brave enough to set a boundary like that—a bullhorn screams, interrupting every conversation in the parking lot as the attention shifts to Ms. P, who's climbed onto the big rock that sits by the soccer net.

"Welcome to Acorn Hill, everyone! Parents, it's time for your final goodbyes. We'll miss you very much, but your campers are ready for the summer of their lives. Our counselors are going to take your groups to our orientation."

The lot bursts into life again as parents give their kids final hugs and retreat to their cars. I hurry over to my group, waving them to gather around as Fitz takes off to do the check-in paperwork for our group with Ms. P.

"Hi, squad," I tell them. "I'm Counselor Ivy. You're all going to be in my group, so we'll be hanging out together during the day, and then splitting up into Cabins Four and Five for your bunks. We'll head over there in a second and have some ice-breakers, but just to get you all thinking about it, we'll need a group name. The only rule is that everyone has to agree on it. So get some ideas going as we head down, okay?"

"Sounds good," Twyla says, and the others nod. I breathe a sigh of relief as we follow Ben's group down the path to the cabins. Now that the parents have retreated and a shred of peace has come back to the parking lot, things are going smoothly.

The campgrounds seemed huge yesterday, but now that they're full of preteens maneuvering all their belongings down the same path, the space feels tighter. I squish my group past Celia's crew and head toward our two cabins.

"Here we are," I say, swinging open the door to the first cabin. The girls traipse forward, clamoring to claim top bunks as they rush in.

Twyla stops short in the doorway, causing a pileup as Emma and Josie crash into her. "Are those *stuffies*?"

I bristle as Vanessa, who'd been the first into the room and quickly scooped a bear into her hands, throws it back onto the mattress she'd claimed like she'd just realized it was a snake. She ducks her head, not making eye contact with Twyla.

"Yeah, that's so weird," she says quickly. "I was just checking it out to see if that's actually what it was."

"I can't believe the camp thinks we're babies," Twyla says with a snort. She hustles to claim the top bunk above the one Vanessa picked. "Nessa and I are friends from school, so we're bunking together."

I make a quick note of the nickname on my clipboard,

busying myself to hide the humiliation of my complete failure, before I scurry to let the boys into their cabin. I ponder hurrying inside to scoop the teddies off their bunks, but worry that'll just make it look sexist, like I only set up stuffies for the girls, so I leave them for the campers to make fun of as they pick their beds. So much for making them feel at home.

"Orientation is in five minutes," I say, standing between the two doorways so both groups can hear me. "Just dump your stuff and we'll head over."

"Ugh, I want to change," Ella whines.

"Yeah," Twyla says, poking her head out. "Don't we have time to unpack?"

"That comes later," I say, glancing down at the schedule tacked to my clipboard. "Don't worry, this afternoon is all about getting settled."

"I'm changing," Ella calls out, rushing back to her duffel.

Frantic, I glance at my watch. What am I supposed to do if my campers won't listen to me? Fitz and his cabin group are already filing into the meeting space. Rynn's group has been in there for ages.

"We really have to get going," I say, a note of panic creeping into my voice. Mercifully, Ella emerges, changed into her summery gear, and Josie and Emma follow her. The boys file out too, leaving us waiting on Twyla and Nessa.

"Girls?" I call toward the cabin. "We have to head over."

Twyla flounces out with an eye roll, and Nessa follows her, playing with the ends of her dark brown ponytail.

"Last year we got to unpack right away."

"We'll have time later," I repeat, but there's not nearly enough authority in my shaky voice.

By the time we make it to the meeting space, Ms. P has already launched into her welcome speech. I shoot Twyla a glare as she starts talking to Nessa, but she doesn't get the hint, so I rush over to her and whisper, "Ms. P is talking, and we need this information."

She ignores me, and a blush creeps into my cheeks. I can feel Rynn watching me, judging, and when I glance over my shoulder, I confirm that her eyes are on me.

"Okay, if you can't stop talking, swap seats with Sammy," I tell her.

She doesn't move to get up, and neither does Sammy. I'm sweating now, heat flooding my face.

"I'll stop, I'll stop," she assures me, but as soon as I go back to stand in the aisle, she's back to chatting with Nessa. I decide the best course of action is to simply pretend I do not see her.

"My next instructions are about laundry. Every year we have a camper who shrinks every article of clothing they own, so please pay attention," Ms. P says from the front of the room, where she's pacing in front of the semicircle of seated campers.

Josie's hand shoots up, and before she's called on, she jumps to her feet to shout her question. "What do we do if that happens?"

"I'll get to questions at the end," Ms. P says, her gaze wandering to the aisle as she searches for Josie's counselor. Who, unfortunately, is me. I motion for Josie to sit down, but she either can't or won't see me.

"But if all our clothes shrink, what do we do?" she asks. Panic hitches her voice, and I feel bad for disavowing her. The poor girl is just nervous.

Inching down the aisle, I reach her in time, before another question comes pouring out.

"That won't happen," I assure her.

"But what if it does?" she asks, her tone teetering on the edge of tears. "I packed all my favorite shirts."

"I'll help you find a solution if it does," I tell her, "but I really don't think it will. I'll help you with laundry if you're nervous."

She nods, and her relief is contagious. I take the win, pretending I don't hear Twyla whispering to Nessa as I scoot away from Josie.

I pull out my phone as I reach the aisle where all the counselors are standing by their groups, dimming the screen so no one notices I'm ignoring the orientation. I've heard all Ms. P's stories a billion times as a camper, and I haven't treated myself to my daily scroll of hell and tragedy yet today. I swipe closed a series of family group chat notifications and dive headfirst into the land of TV recaps and breakup bad takes. A new episode of Ally's stupid show aired last night, so the fandom is out in full force. Unfortunately for me, her character had a phone call or something with her girlfriend. There's some kind of tragic star-crossed lovers thing happening on her show where she can't return to Earth and her girlfriend can't leave. Sci-fi is so not my thing, so even though I faithfully watched every episode, I still only half remember the world-building, let alone the plot. But I know the fans lose their minds when Ally's character gets to talk to her girlfriend. Even more so now that Ally is merrily single and available for dating her costar. I pick at the scab of my heartbreak with every new post and almost miss Ms. P telling us to dismiss our campers back to their cabins for unpacking before lunch.

As we file out, I finally hear what Twyla and Nessa have been talking about this whole time.

"It was *so* cute," Twyla is saying. "I hope they get another phone call next week. Not that we can watch until the end of camp."

Nessa groans. "How am I supposed to live without it?"

My acid-pumping heart is back in action. Nausea floods my stomach. Do tweens watch *Telephone Hour*?

"What are you guys talking about?" I ask.

"This show, *Telephone Hour*," Twyla tells me, treating me to a confirmation of my worst fears in spite of what Melody, my therapist, always tells me about catastrophizing. "We're obsessed with it. Allyson Hendricks is amazing."

"I sent her a DM after her breakup," Nessa confesses.

Twyla giggles. "Ness! She's not even gonna read it."

"Maybe not, but I want her to know I support her," Nessa says as the two head off back to the cabins. "I can't imagine what I would do if I broke up with my boyfriend."

I stare after them, trembling. So not only do the tweens watch the stupid show, they're all on Ally's side?

It's so unfair. She gets to log off the internet. She can afford to buy strong enough walls to block out all the hot takes, with

47

hired hands to screen the comments for her and spin the narrative in her favor. It's someone's whole job to make sure she comes out of this discourse with her fandom intact, to spin the story in her favor, so that everyone's telling her version. There's nothing between me and the searing comments left under every edit and reposted article and new theory about the show. No publicist to field the callous cruelty that's been thrown my way since *her* publicist sent the press release to her favorite outlet.

Another fear occurs to me. If the kids are fans of Ally's, they might follow her accounts. And if they follow her, they'll have seen all the pictures of us from when we were happy. Sharing frozen yogurt cups, kissing at the top of hiking trails, traveling to see each other between shoots. I'm all over her feed, and last time I checked (two minutes ago), she hadn't taken the posts down. Our relationship history is plastered all over her profile for all to see, my face on full display.

An even more frightening thought occurs to me. What if Twyla recognized me not from camp brochure materials, but from Ally's social media?

I tug at the ends of my hair, which has mercifully returned to its natural brown state after years of being bleached a bright blond I've come to seriously regret. Call it Trying to Fit In with Hollywood Syndrome, I guess. But at least I look different now than I do in the social media chronicles of our relationship.

Still, what if they connect the dots?

I can't let that happen. The mark I leave on this camp will not be "that freshly dumped counselor who let her group run amok during orientation." At least Rynn is so perennially offline,

I can count on her to know nothing about *Telephone Hour,* let alone that its star has just dumped her high school sweetheart.

I shade my eyes from the midmorning sun, watching my group split into their cabins. At least they're all getting along. Maybe bonding over how dumb my cabin decor ideas were will help them form faster friendships. Still, I hate handing Rynn a win already.

As if she heard my thoughts, Rynn sidles up to me. "Texting on the job much?"

I turn to glare at her, though the eye full of sun I get as I face her turns it into more of a peaky squint. "Are you going to be on my case all summer?"

"Probably," Rynn says airily. "Seriously, though, that seemed rough. You okay?"

I grit my teeth. We could barely agree to keep things professional yesterday. There's no way she's progressed to actually caring about my emotional well-being. She just wants to rub how badly I did in my face while keeping her plausible deniability intact.

"Doing great, thanks," I say, trying to keep my tone neutral. "You seem to have a good group. Easy."

The last word slips out unintentionally, a shield slipping over the feeling of inadequacy that's been haunting me since I saw how effortlessly she faced the chaos of the morning.

"My group is anything but easy," Rynn says smoothly. "I just know how to handle them."

"I know how to handle my group, I just can't handle you right now," I snarl. It's leaving behind all that promised professionalism in the dust. But between my rowdy group and their apparent fixation on my girlfriend—my *ex*-girlfriend—I have no time for Rynn's jibes about how much better she is at this than me. I have to get their minds off the show and keep them there. So without another word to my former best friend, I rush up the hill after them, leaving her looking vaguely stunned behind me.

4

AllysonHendricksOfficial [51 weeks ago]: happiest anniversary to @IvyRaines, the best girlfriend I could ever ask for. From our actual fetus days, freaking out about our seventh-grade science pop quizzes and sneaking Twizzlers from CVS into our town's two-room movie theater, to the red carpet at this season's premiere, I'm so freaking grateful I get to call you mine.

IvyRaines: love you to the moon and back xxxx

CarlyWhittell: lmaooo the second pic of Ivy is unreal. I can't believe what babies you were when you met!

LadsWhoGame: absolute couple goals

TeleFanHour: we stan middle school sweethearts

GeorgiaEfferts: my boyfriend and I met in seventh grade too! Happy anniversary!

THE PINES MAKE EVERYTHING SMELL PEACEFUL. IN the early-morning air, everything is quiet, and the bubbled-over excitement of the first day has eased into misty sleepiness that blends in with the blurred-out edges of the sky. I gather my group onto the parking lot asphalt, their sneakers slapping against the silence of the morning. They rub their eyes and stifle yawns to cover for how late they stayed up last night. I can't blame them. This is our pre-breakfast first-day meeting, and I didn't wake up early enough to sneak to the coffee machine before gathering my campers. In my noncaffeinated state, I'm seriously regretting the deal I made with Fitz last night. He ran the night activities, giving me a break, in exchange for me doing this. Now the bags under my eyes are large enough to declare independence from the rest of my face.

Twyla stands across the circle from me, her pinkie entwined with Nessa's. Their hands sway sleepily in the space between them. Elliott, the only one whose eyes are already bright, makes a crack at Wally, who summons the energy to chuckle in response. I take a deep breath, the pine-spiced air a small comfort against the already overwhelming task of bringing this group together.

"Good morning," I say, and I get a few half-hearted greetings back. "I gave you that homework assignment yesterday. Did anyone come up with any group names?"

"The Chicken Nuggets!" Elliott suggests.

"Ew, no," Twyla says immediately. "I'm not being a nugget all summer."

I roll my weight from the balls of my feet to the heels. "We all have to agree for a name to fly. But let's also hear each other out."

"Well, I think we should be the Camp Girlies," Twyla says.

"What? No way," Sammy protests.

"It's cute," Twyla argues. She shoots a look at Nessa, who nods but doesn't summon the courage to join the fray.

"What about the Stargazers?" Wally suggests in a voice that sounds like it should come from a toddler ducked behind his mother's skirt.

"That's so cute," Nessa says. This earns her a shocked glare from Twyla.

"What do you mean? You said you liked Camp Girlies!"

"I just . . . I mean, yeah, I like Camp Girlies, but Sammy—"

"Let's do a vote," Twyla says, slicing her hand into the air above her head. "All for Camp Girlies?"

I'm rooted to the spot as Nessa lifts her hand in the air, followed by Ella. When it comes to the whole fight, flight, or freeze thing, there's no fight in my body. Fleeing this conflict is obviously not an option, given how close we are to a *Lord of the Flies* situation even under my dubious supervision, so my body has gone with growing roots instead.

The coolness of the early-morning mist is gone, replaced with a flaming heat that licks my cheeks as I melt under the pressure of this argument. Whenever my sisters fight, I blend in with our surroundings and wait until it's over, a craft I honed in the months leading up to my parents' divorce. Now, though, it's my literal job to step in. I toe around the edges of the fight like it's the rebounding tip of a too-high diving board, gauging how far the fall will be.

"We're not voting," I say, clearing my throat. My stomach squirms against the drop—the fall feels as far as I feared it would be. Ella drops her hand, and after a moment Twyla reluctantly lowers hers too. "It has to be unanimous. Does anyone have any other suggestions?"

I just want this to be over, but if I show up to breakfast with the only unnamed group of campers, Rynn will come at me with more preening disguised as support. I've had all the smugness I can handle for the week.

No one has any other suggestions, and my brain is still too busy reeling from the panic of presiding over the summer's first confrontation to come up with anything clever, though. Huffing a sigh at the mental image of Rynn's smirk, I give in.

"Let's keep thinking and reconvene at lunch," I say. "I don't want to waste too much time and miss getting a good table for breakfast."

Twyla sighs, and I hear her mutter something to Nessa. Her tone doesn't sound particularly kind, but I can't make out her words. Besides, I'm still trembling internally from stalling the first fight of the day. I can't handle stepping into another one before I've even had my breakfast.

Nessa falls into step beside me. "When can I use my phone? I want to call my boyfriend."

I shrug as I hold open the door to the dining hall for her. "You can check it out during free play." Ms. P compromised parents' desire to call their kids with her desire to give them an unplugged summer by setting specific times when campers can check out their cell phones from the main office.

Inside the dining hall, I discover that two groups have beaten us to breakfast. Ben is leading his cabin group in a rendition of "Good Morning, Good Day" from *She Loves Me* that is entirely too spirited for the early hour, even if we are at theater camp. At least he has amazing taste. Rynn, of course, is already halfway through her breakfast of Corn Flakes, her campers around the table in various degrees of wakefulness. I claim the table across the dining hall from her, but it's still close enough that I can see her roll her eyes at me as I sit.

"Get thee to the buffet line," I tell my group, and they scamper off to join Ben's kids. Ella and Sammy even start singing as they reach him. Traitors.

I make my way to the gluten-free corner of the dining hall, where a fresh batch of sweet, sweet GF pancakes are steaming in a tray. Unfortunately, there's no way to reach my personal corner of heaven without walking past Rynn.

"Good morning so far?" she asks me, her smirk steady on her face as she takes a sip of tea. "We came up with a group name *and* a group cheer. We're the Birdies, and what do we say?"

"Bye, bye," her group cheers in unison.

Twyla, who's last in the breakfast line, has the nerve to giggle. "We should do a cheer too! Once we come up with a name."

I grit my teeth as Rynn smiles—no, that's not quite the right word. It's more like baring her teeth.

"Oh, have you not come up with a name yet?"

She's staring right at me, but Twyla answers anyway.

"Nope. We couldn't agree. Counselor Ivy said we can try again after lunch."

Can the earth swallow me whole now? Just straight to the core so I can melt in the iron. Anything would be better than the laughter sizzling in Rynn's gaze.

"Counselor Ivy didn't have a single idea of her own?" she asks.

"I think it's best if the kids come up with their own name," I snap. Her words curdle in my veins, but her petty jibes do more than bug me. It's like they bring me back to my sixth-grade body, all knobby knees and angst too powerful for my tiny, pre-growth-spurt frame. The way she rubs my face in my nonstop failures as a counselor so far brings all that prepubescent anger rushing back to the surface. It's as if I've kept a little vault of tween girl rage in my chest that the sight of Rynn unlocks, letting it all spill back to the surface, fresh as the day I brewed it.

"Totally," Twyla says. "Except no one liked my idea."

The thought of tween girl rage makes me look at her in a new light. What has Twyla brought to camp with her from her home life, her school community, her family and friend dynamics? What feelings have all my campers brought with them, packed alongside their character shoes and sunscreen? I want to be a teacher so I can help kids grow up, help them navigate the minefield of tweenhood that chewed me up and spat me back out again when I was their age. Now that I'm faced with the reality of tweenhood right in front of me, in the bright eyes of this girl who's done nothing but derail my plans since she got here, I have no idea how to actually go about it.

How am I supposed to connect with these kids *and* get them

to like me *and* make sure they get along with each other *and* actually get to all the stuff the camp has planned? All while making sure no one realizes I was just dumped by cheesy sci-fi's favorite actress?

I used to hate Rynn's lack of social media, seeing how impossible it made my attempts to find out what she was up to after our split, but now I wish everyone would take a page out of her book and get off the internet.

Minimum wage isn't enough for this.

I force myself to inhale, breathing deep to cut off my panic spiral before I burst into tears in front of Rynn. That's one unfortunate part of my personality I haven't outgrown since I've known her. Tears come out no matter what I'm feeling, and they're the last thing I want Rynn or my campers to see. So I swallow hard and brush past Rynn, who's busy bonding with *my* camper, to those pancakes.

AFTER BREAKFAST MY GROUP HAS OUR FIRST CLASS of the summer. I glance at my schedule, and immediately send all my spiciest mental curses Ms. P's way. Because she's scheduled Fitz and me to partner with another group for improv first thing this morning, and of course it's Rynn's group. Which means that, given how today is going so far, I'm going to get to fail right in front of her.

The universe has truly forsaken me.

Energized by breakfast, my group skips down the grassy path

to the dance studio, which is housed in a worn cabin behind the first aid room. The outside might look like it's falling apart as much as the rest of the cabins on the campground, but inside the window AC unit is actually working, and the floor has been laid with clean dance flooring. As far as Acorn Hill is concerned, it's state of the art.

The improv/dance teacher, a broad-shouldered woman with sleek purple hair, waves us into the studio and guides the kids into a seated semicircle on the floor. We counselors teach most of the classes ourselves, but for something with as much potential for injury as dance, Ms. P hired an actual professional. Celia told us all that getting to shadow Ms. Zheng is one of the reasons she came to this camp, so I can only assume she's great.

"Hi, squad. I'm Ms. Zheng, and I'll be teaching you all about improv, ballet, tap, and jazz this summer. I'll also be choreographing some moves for your musical, so we're going to have a lot of fun together," she tells the kids.

Nessa is sitting with her back pin straight, as though someone has pressed a ruler against her spine. It's clear dance is her *thing*. I make a mental note, though given that genetics blessed me with Mom's two left feet, I'm not sure how to bond with her over it.

The first half hour of class passes inoffensively. Ms. Zheng runs an icebreaker game, and I pretend to have to go to the bathroom before I can be called upon to perform a silly noise in front of the whole group. I'm all about theater, but even I have to draw some lines in the sand, and it turns out embarrassing myself in front of the ten tweens who are already struggling to see me as their leader is one of them.

When I come back, Ms. Zheng has gathered everyone around her laptop. "The next game is a really fun one. I'll be showing a clip from a show and then assigning a group of you to finish the scene as you see fit. Who wants to go first?"

Wally, Arlo, and a girl named Phoebe from Rynn's group go first, deciding to set their rendition of a sitcom scene on an active volcano. They're rewarded with peals of laughter from their audience, and then Ms. Zheng assigns Twyla, Ella, and Elliott to the next scene.

When she hits her space bar and the screen jerks to life, my heart flatlines. It's a scene from *Telephone Hour*. Ally fills the screen, the camera tight on her face as she maneuvers her spaceship through an asteroid field. The surprise sight of her face squeezes my heart, pulsing out a message in its fist. *You're! Not! Over! Her!*

It's true. Because all I can think as the scene plays is that I remember the day she shot this episode. It's an old one, from last season, back when we were together and happy that way. I'd visited the set, watched her fly across a green screen, cheered when she landed every time. The rest of the cast thought I was the biggest dork, but I didn't care. I could tell she liked my cheering because she couldn't help but grin a moment too soon, ruining every single take. The director banished me to her trailer, where I prepped two mugs of hot chocolate to surprise her with when she finished shooting. We sipped them later as we swapped stories about the days since we'd last seen each other, and then we celebrated being in the same room for the first time in months by making out on her couch.

I hate how happy the memory still is. There was no trace, then, of the anger and heartbreak to come. All the sadness I see now is retrospective, but the happiness I felt that day is perfectly preserved in my heart, like a wildflower dried between its pages.

Blissfully unaware of the turmoil churning away in my heart, Twyla squeals when she sees who she'll be playing. "I love this show."

"It's the best," Phoebe agrees. "Did you hear she just broke up with her girlfriend?"

"Ugh, yes, it's so sad," Nessa says. "I thought it was so cute that she was dating her middle school sweetheart. I mean, it's super inspiring for me and my boyfriend."

"Not me," Phoebe says. "I ship her and Becca Wallis so hard."

Because of course Rynn's camper sees it that way.

I stare at them as they go back and forth, crossing my fingers in the folds of my skirt. Please, universe, if there's a shred of sympathy for me left, don't let them recognize me. Please.

Then I catch Rynn's eye. She's taking in my panicked eyes and red-tinted cheeks, and her brain is whirring entirely too fast for my liking. Her eyes widen, and she lets out a gasp. I give the tiniest shake of my head—the most earnest plea I'd ever let myself give her—and she bites down on her lower lip.

It's Twyla who puts it together next. She's stopped listening to Nessa and the other camper, her eyes volleying between Rynn and me like she's watching a tennis match. And then it's her turn to gasp.

"*THAT'S* where I know you from!" she shouts.

Nessa follows her gaze, and before I can stop it from happening, the words come tumbling out of her mouth.

"Wait, Counselor . . . *Ivy*—you're Allyson Hendricks's girlfriend?"

"*Ex*-girlfriend," insists Phoebe as she sizes me up. "Oh god, um . . . sorry, about what I said. I didn't . . ."

She trails off. Though I'm reeling from the shock of my worst nightmare unfolding before my all-too-awake eyes, I can't say I blame her. When it comes to the breakups we participate in through the comments section, it's easy to forget there are real people attached to the other end of the gossip. It's not this girl's fault that she's being confronted with the flesh-and-blood heartbreak she's only seen as on-screen entertainment until now.

"No, I'm—" But I have no idea what to follow this up with. Thanks to Ally's verified internet presence, they can confirm their suspicions as soon as one of them checks out their cell phone to "call their parents."

I can't believe I used to think all her sappy anniversary posts were cute. The one she posted in eighth grade, our very first anniversary, was so saccharine it made me cry. By our second anniversary, her follower count had skyrocketed thanks to *Telephone Hour* finding its fan base in its second season, and the comments were chock-full of overfamiliar fans giggling conspiratorially at my braces in our first date picture. Still, I saw through them to the heart of the post, to the love I never thought I'd lose.

"It's okay," I tell Phoebe. It's not her fault Ally lifted me up to the world as the love of her life—her adorable middle school sweetheart who gave her an oh-so-down-to-earth image—only to publicly drop me, leaving me to drown in the depths of the comments section.

"Let's move on," Rynn says smoothly. "Counselor Ivy's life outside of camp is none of y'all's business."

At least Phoebe has the decency to blush. I catch Rynn's eye and give her a small smile, the best thanks I can muster while my feelings are still in a full rolling boil. Ms. Zheng seems old enough to be free from the Internet Drama of the Day, a life stage I envy so hard right now, and her eyes flit from me to the campers before she shrugs and tells them to carry on with the scene. I'm left to watch Twyla perform a perfect impression of my ex, down to the way she raises her eyebrows when she asks a question.

It's unnerving enough that I move to the window, pretending that I spot a lost camper or something. Fitz follows me, leaning casually against the windowsill as he ducks his head to make eye contact.

"Sounds like you left some stuff out of your life story last night, huh?" he teases.

I'd be annoyed if anybody else said it, but Fitz has such an easy way about him and says it in a light tone that doesn't carry any hint of a loaded comment, and I can't help but smile.

"Just a few details."

"That Allyson Hendricks girl is missing out on some well-toasted s'mores," he says, and I roll my eyes to hide my laugh.

Rynn watches me from across the studio, and I can feel the questions in her eyes, but I play the idiot and refuse to look at her for the rest of class.

⁂

WHOEVER SAID IT'S BETTER TO LOVE AND LOSE THAN never love at all has some serious explaining to do. People who never love at all may not get to know how Ally's nose wrinkles in laughter when you kiss it, but they also do not have to know what it's like when an army of ten twelve-year-olds runs a day-long excavation into the ruins of your relationship.

"What was the set of *Telephone Hour* like?" Twyla asks dreamily as I lead the group from their theater games class to lunch.

"Crowded," I answer flatly.

At the end of free play, Ella wants to know if Ally is a good kisser.

"Can't say, sorry, I signed an NDA." This is not true, but it makes Ella's eyes go wide.

Nessa shyly asks what it was like to be in love when I hold the dance studio door open for her to head into our character dance class. "I just want to know when the time is right to tell my boyfriend I love him, I mean."

I stare at her for a long while before sighing.

Like an earthquake, I want to tell her. Like the whole world flips over at once, and all I could do was cling to her as I tried to find my footing. I guess I should've known it would pass, that the earth would eventually stop rolling, leaving everything slightly out of place in the newfound stillness.

But that feels slightly morbid to say to her bright eyes, so instead I shrug and pass her off with some vague platitude about enjoying the moment instead of worrying about getting to the next step.

By the time we wave the campers off to bed, I'm grateful to see the backs of them. Between Twyla and Sammy's incessant arguing about the group name and the stream of questions I can't seem to quell, nothing about today lived up to my camp dreams.

I wait until the cabin is filled with light snores to pull out my phone, squinting as it lights up my face in the otherwise dark cabin. There's a bunch of Ally updates from the embarrassing Google Alert I haven't disabled yet, seventeen notifications in the family group chat, and an email waiting from Ms. P—a calendar invite to interview for the musical director job tomorrow afternoon. I hit yes with a trembling finger.

After today, with my campers wide-eyed not in awe at my fantastic counseloring ability but with speculation at my dating life, it's more important than ever that I get this job. Being a counselor won't be enough—if I leave at the end of the summer having merely shepherded these kids from one class to the next, all I'll ever be remembered for is being that one camper turned counselor who got dumped by a celebrity.

The musical is my chance to connect with the campers in a more meaningful way—which I desperately need to do, given what a shit go I've been making of it so far. And it'd be something tangible to leave behind here, a legacy of sorts for this place that helped raise me.

This camp is a part of my life Ally never touched. Being her girlfriend, and now her ex-girlfriend, doesn't get to claim my identity here, too.

I switch from my email to my notes app, where the sad little draft I started last night waits for me. I still have no idea what I want to say to her. I just know I don't want to leave it on the last note we had—the one where I ugly-cried in her face as she patiently and calmly told me she didn't love me anymore.

A text notification comes through the family group chat. Lacey sent an eye roll emoji that I'm pretty sure is supposed to be the caption to a photo, but no picture comes through to accompany it. They must have bad service.

It occurs to me that I could take this text drafting process from the notes app to the group chat. I know Lacey has good text flirting game because her college situationships are always blowing up her phone. But the idea of telling her that I'm still hung up on Ally, let alone that I want to text her, is so embarrassing that I put my phone face down on the splintery cabin floor and pretend to myself that sleep will come easily after such a busy day.

It does not.

Ext. Xolfarat Main Street—Day

Artis and Milo walk down the busy marketplace street. Around them, sellers shout out the wares they're selling: everything from secondhand spaceship parts and sand dune riders to local fruits and vegetables.

ARTIS

What do you think is the closest thing they have to a peach?

MILO

We're here to find . . .

(beat as he checks the business card)

Dr. Grains and trade Anklor's amulet before the Intergalactic Force kills us for even having it, and you're wondering about *peaches*?

ARTIS

It's summertime on Earth right now. And it's been years since I've had a peach.

Milo doesn't respond, but he takes her hand as the two reach a run-down jewelry stand run by a young woman with white hair. DR. GRAINS.

INTERVIEW PREP:

Wear a non-embarrassing outfit free of stains? Check.

Rehearse answers in the mirror while popping an unfortunately placed forehead zit? Check.

Avoid checking social media to not set off a giant panic spiral moments before said interview? Big fat failure.

All Becca's posted is a photo of two coffee mugs, a tiny apple tart, and two blurred-out script covers sitting atop a blue-tiled café table. A hand curls around one of the white ceramic mugs. *Just a line reading kind of day,* the caption assures us.

Simple enough, but the comments section is aflame with speculation. And, lucky me, she cross-posted it to every platform she has, so no matter what corner of the internet I run to, there it is waiting for me. Making sure I'm haunted by the knowledge that Ally spent all last night holed up in some adorable coffee shop, downing an apple tart and drinking coffee with her way-hotter-than-me costar. I mean, the girl got cast on a show run by a network that might as well rename itself Impossibly Beautiful Children Star in Corny Shows. And now Ally's manicured hand is prominently featured in Becca's latest photo. All the same fans who used to coo over my middle school dinner dance photos are grasping at each other over the thrill of the *will they, won't they* of it all.

67

And with all that buzzing in my head, I'm supposed to deliver a coherent enough vision for this production of *Peter Pan* to land me a job?

This breakup is really the gift that keeps on giving.

Mercifully, Ms. P nods a lot as I tell her about my experience as the drama teacher's assistant for my high school's spring musical. I only trip over my words twice, and I cover by faking a cough. A little too convincingly, as I find myself sucking on a cough drop as Ms. P explains the responsibilities of the role.

"I want to make sure you have all the break time you need, and for the most part rehearsal will happen while your group is in sessions. But there may be some extra hours, especially during tech week."

"That's fine," I say, crossing my legs. It's a mistake: the ancient couch I've settled into in the main office swallows me whole, and I spend an undignified minute rescuing myself from the cushions. "I'm excited about it, actually. I want to be all-in on the camp experience this summer, and this was always my favorite part of it as a kid."

Ms. P smiles. "I thought you would be. And I think this could be a great opportunity for the camp, too."

Well, that goes straight to my head. I can't believe she thinks me directing the musical could be an opportunity for Acorn Hill. But then again, my takes on musicals are very good.

"Honestly, the camp is in some financial trouble," Ms. P says, leaning closer to me across the coffee table. "We've had low enrollment for a few years, and we've gotten by with a slimmer staff to lower the budget, but it isn't sustainable. This year we're hoping to use the musical as a showcase to attract more local campers."

"So it's gotta be special," I say, beaming as I meet her eye.

"Absolutely." Ms. P nods. "And I think you could really attract a new audience, too. What with your . . . presence, and all."

Time to be brought back down to earth. Of course. This isn't about my impeccable taste in musical theater or my natural teaching ability. Like everything else, it's about Ally. Even here, my name is synonymous with *Allyson Hendricks's girlfriend*.

Ex. Ex ex ex.

It seems as though my name has always been entwined with hers. I was a quiet kid at school, and when we started dating, everyone knew us as *Ally and her girlfriend*. And then she became the face of televised sci-fi and *her girlfriend* became my national moniker. I thought not being alongside her anymore might help disentangle us, but I've just fallen into her shadow.

Ms. P must read my face because she smiles as she adds, "I'm so excited about everything you said. I'll let you know as soon as I decide."

There's nothing left for me to do but nod, dismissed.

I shut the office door gently behind me and make my way back up the dirt path to the cafeteria. Where, of course, I run into Rynn. The morning sun lights up her face, teasing out the golden undertones of her brown hair. Summer is bringing out her freckles again, and they warm her face with familiarity, the memories of all the summers we spent together smattered across her nose, and for one ridiculous moment, I want to lean on her like I once did. I want to tell her about my interview, and how

I've been reduced to nothing more than Ally's shadow, discon-
nected from her body like I'm living out the first act of *Peter Pan*.

But the thought of the interview reminds me that, no matter
what our history is, right now we're pitted against each other.

So instead, I force my face into a polite smile as we pass each
other. "Good luck."

"Thanks," she says, but when she turns her head to meet
my eyes, all the yearning for what came before floods me again,
until I tear my eyes off her and keep walking away.

⚘

I REJOIN FITZ AT THE FIELD, WHERE I ABANDONED HIM
with our group. The large grassy expanse behind the dining hall
is where we're supposed to run theater games for an hour before
shuttling the kids to a singing class. Fitz has introduced them to
a game of his own invention, Snack Attack, which, from what I
can gather as I join them, entails embodying a character inspired
by a snack food and then carrying out an argument with your
scene partner. Ella and Arlo are currently battling it out as Right
Twix and Left Twix.

"Well, I'm always *right*," Ella insists, and Fitz hoots with
laughter.

"And I'm always *left* to win," Arlo counters. Fitz leads a round
of applause as they take bows and return to the seated circle the
kids have formed in the grass.

Twyla and Nessa are up next. They bound into the center of
the circle, facing off as a Snickers and a Starburst.

I walk around the circle to find Fitz. He grins at me when I settle next to him in the grass.

"This game is great," I tell him.

"Inspired by my current starvation," he says. "The fact that afternoon snack is not formally recognized on the camp schedule is a travesty."

"On this we agree," I say.

"What if our next theater game was making cinnamon rolls?" Fitz asks.

"Are we allowed to do that?"

He shrugs. "If we clean up, I don't see why not. And if we never ask, no one will tell us no. And the kids will love it."

He's right; they would. How does he come up with this stuff? I'm still scrambling to wrap my head around being in charge of this many kids and getting them to follow basic instructions, and he's already settled into his role as cool dad counselor.

When Twyla declares herself the winner of Snack Attack, Fitz leaps to his feet. "Alright, next we're going to the kitchen."

"Why?" asks Sammy.

"Because I'm hungry."

Unable to argue with the logic in this, Sammy and the rest follow Fitz to the dining hall, where Fitz charms the kitchen staff into showing him where the flour is kept. They even take pity on me and track down their gluten-free flour and xanthan gum. Soon the whole place is filled with giggling and the spiced scent of cinnamon as the kids take turns frosting a bun.

"Can you take a picture?" Nessa asks me, posing with her bun. "I want to send it to my boyfriend."

"This is the best," Sammy says as he helps Fitz slide a tray full of our puffy creations into the oven. "How long till they're ready?"

"Probably after singing," I say, glancing at the wall clock. We're about to be late.

I'm met with a chorus of groans, because of course I am. It takes Fitz setting a timer and promising to bring the pastries straight to class when they're ready to avoid a complete mutiny.

I follow the group to the outdoor amphitheater where today's singing lessons are taking place, doing my best not to let the way the kids flock to Fitz get to me. It's good, I tell myself. They're having the best summer of their young lives, as they should be.

I just don't have a lot to do with it.

<u>Ext. Lake on Moonslate—Day</u>

Artis and Milo walk alongside the lake. They are not speaking to each other.
After several moments, Artis rolls her eyes.

ARTIS

Stop giving me the silent treatment. It's not my fault.

MILO

You're the one not talking to me!
Artis cannot argue with this. She looks back at the place where their rendezvous shuttle should've been. Nothing is there except that same perfect circle of ash, marking its takeoff.

ARTIS

We're going to miss the Telephone Hour.

MILO

It's okay. We'll get them next week.

We missed last week too! The swampangel attack, remember?

(beat)

Hemilia will think I'm dead.

I WAKE UP TO A TEXT FROM MS. P AND SKIP STRAIGHT to the main office without even stopping for breakfast. There's only one reason she'd want to meet with me, and it's to offer me the job. I'm sure of it. Director's chair, here I come.

When I see Rynn loitering outside the main office, I skid to a halt. Maybe she's just here for a hot chocolate, I tell myself. The fog seems to have followed us from San Francisco and the mornings have been unseasonably cold. I eye her warily as I pause by the office door.

"Good morning," I snarl. Professionally.

"Hello," she says back, her teeth gritted in a manner that can only be called unprofessional. "Here for the coffee station?"

"Ms. P texted me," I say, flashing my phone screen at her. "She wants to meet."

Rynn frowns, her stubby fingers weaving into her ponytail. "Me too."

"Ah, that's too ba— Wait, what?"

Rynn waves her phone screen in my face, mimicking my earlier enthusiasm. I force a smile, baring all my teeth at her.

"Then I guess we're meeting together," I say, arms stiff at my sides. "Joyous."

"I bet we're in trouble," Rynn snaps. "I told you to be professional."

"What? Why would we be in trouble?" I ask, taken aback. Nothing has happened between us. Not unless you count her basically outing me as Ally's ex to Twyla. But even I know she didn't do it on purpose, and I was recently voted Least Likely to Give Rynn Any Grace at All.

"I don't know," Rynn says, throwing her hands up in the air, "but I'm sure it's your fault."

"Whatever helps you cope," I mutter.

Our spat is interrupted by Ms. P, who comes rushing up the hill with a set of keys. Broccoli runs after her, his tail wagging steadily with every step they take together. She huffs to catch her breath as she unlocks the door and waves us in. "Anyone want anything to drink?"

I could go for a tea, but I shake my head. Now that Rynn has planted the idea that we might be in trouble, I want to get this conversation over with as soon as possible. Rynn, continual traitor that she is, agrees to a cup of coffee, and I wait for ages on the faded couch as Ms. P struggles to revive the coffee maker. Broccoli hops up next to me, stretching to take up most of the couch, my thigh serving as his pillow. I scratch him behind the ears as I wait.

When the two at last have steaming mugs in front of them, adding their rings to the array of stains on the coffee table, Ms. P begins.

"I was so impressed with both of your interviews," she says, and my heart sinks. Are we going to find out who gets the job in front of each other? I can't handle losing this job to Rynn with her right here. I'm exactly that experience away from launching myself into space.

"I think you both bring such important visions to the role. Rynn, you have the experience at this camp, and Ivy, your musical theater experience is unparalleled."

Rynn and I exchange looks, and I can tell that for once we're on the same page. Utter confusion tinged with extreme worry at where this is headed.

"I think the musical would be best served with you two co-directing," Ms. P says. She smiles as she does, as if she hasn't just detonated a massive hole right into my plans for turning this summer around.

Codirect? With Rynn? The same girl who can't stop taunting me with what a bad job I'm doing this summer? I wouldn't trust her with a penny I found on a sidewalk, and we're supposed to collaborate?

Ms. P is watching us expectantly. I don't dare look Rynn's way again. I can't handle reading her expression when all my focus right now is going toward not arguing with Ms. P. Broccoli must sense my agitation because he lifts his head to try to lick my chin. I pat him gently away from my face.

"What do you think?" Ms. P asks. She clearly wasn't expecting her job offer to be met with tense silence.

"Can I have some time to think about it?" I manage. Turning down the job feels like an idiotic move, but agreeing to work with Rynn might be a worse one.

"Oh." Ms. P nods, her slightly raised eyebrows betraying her surprise. "Sure. Of course you can. Let me know by the end of the day?"

Rynn and I nod as we stand and make for the door. I keep not looking at her as we walk side by side to the dining hall. The only sounds are the early-morning birds rustling in the trees above us. Their song only seems to emphasize our silence.

"One of us should turn it down," Rynn says at last.

"So generous of you to offer," I say. She rolls her eyes at me.

"Just an idea." She strides ahead of me, her footsteps crunching the short gravel pathway leading up to the dining hall.

"I'm not turning this job down for you to have it," I snap.

She yanks open the door to the dining hall, and I stalk through. In truth, I have no idea what I'm going to do. This job is my dream come true, but the way Ms. P has offered it to me, it's laced with nightmares.

I WAS LOOKING FORWARD TO A DAY WITHOUT RYNN. Time alone—or, well, as alone as one can ever be in a camp full of eleven-year-olds desperate to know more about my love life and a Fitz desperate to know where to find his next snack—to make my decision.

I really have to start reading the schedule before breakfast. We're slated for an afternoon dance class with Rynn's group. The morning singing class offers no respite within which to mull over my options. Between Sammy's off-key howling and Twyla sneaking away from the group every chance she gets to ask me yet another question about *Telephone Hour,* it's a miracle I make it through the class with my brain intact, let alone functioning enough to make such an important decision. I think about making my escape at lunch, but I'm thwarted by Ella complaining to me about how Nessa won't stop bragging about her boyfriend.

As if my own love life wasn't dramatic enough, now I have to contend with the dating dynamics of tween girls. I have no idea what to do about this latest installment, so I settle for telling Ella that she should join a different conversation if she doesn't like the one she's in. I have no idea if this was the right move, but I'm too busy stressing about this musical to start a separate panic about it.

And then, with barely enough time to down my fries, which the chef has assured me are dipped in a separate fryer from the onion rings, it's time for dance class.

This also coincides with Fitz's afternoon break time, because the universe loves me just that much. He cheerily waves me off as he makes his way to the main office, with no worries except how long it will take him to raid the snack counter, while I shepherd our group to the dance studio alongside Rynn.

Ms. Zheng welcomes us into the studio by announcing that today's class will be a dance battle. "Let's have the day groups face off and bring your best moves."

Rynn flashes me a smirk as she joins her group on the right side of the studio. Ms. Zheng starts the music, an upbeat hip-hop number I'm sure to trip over when it's my turn to join the fray. I start contemplating a bathroom break when one of Rynn's campers cheers that the counselors should kick things off.

Who knew an eleven-year-old could so easily destroy what's left of my emotional well-being?

Rynn eagerly hops to the middle of the room. I cringe as I watch her feet move so easily under her. She's always been a better dancer than me. She showed me up at every middle school dance we attended together in sixth grade, and I have no doubt she'll show me up now.

Especially when I enter the fray by tripping over my own feet and stumbling to the center of the room. I try to play it off as intentional as I throw in a spin, but that just makes me dizzy. Ms. Zheng declares Rynn the winner, and no one even has the decency to act surprised. Her group goes wild, cheering and jumping around her as she rejoins them for a round of high fives.

Meanwhile, Twyla offers me a half-hearted pat on the shoulder, while Sammy cranes his neck to look around the studio. "Where's Counselor Fitz? Bet he'd rock this."

"He's on break," I mutter. The worst part is, I have no doubt Fitz would be amazing.

As it is, in spite of Nessa performing some impressive ballet-inspired moves and Sammy doing a semi-decent headstand, Rynn's group wins with a chorus of whoops and a group high five followed by their *Bye Bye Birdie*–inspired cheer.

Rynn is all smirks as we walk our kids out of the studio.

"To the winner go the spoils?" she asks.

"If by spoils you mean bragging rights over a bunch of kids, sure," I respond evenly.

"I meant the job, and you know it. My skills in there prove I'm the better candidate."

"Beating me in a dance competition is hardly proof of skill," I point out.

She laughs. "Ouch. Need some ice for that self-burn?"

"Need some extra brain cells to do better than that joke you stole from the internet?"

She's rescued from the trouble of responding by Twyla, who interrupts to ask if she can check out her phone. I nod since we have a free play break until dinner and take her to the storage room. It's a large enough cabin, but a tight space given how many cabinets are stuffed in there. The one by the door houses camper cell phones, which they can only use at certain times of day to be in touch with their parents. I fill in the check-out form and unlock my group's drawer, fishing Twyla's bright yellow phone case from its depths and handing it to her.

She's supposed to text her parents only. I don't have it in me to supervise her actual phone use, which is my first mistake. Because soon she's gasping, "I thought so."

"Everything okay?" I ask. So naively. Because I actually think she's texting with her family.

Turns out she was checking Instagram. Specifically Ally's Instagram. Because she's scrolled far enough to the last post Ally made for our anniversary.

Posted fifty-two weeks ago.

"Today would've been your anniversary?" she asks.

I blink at her, momentarily confused. She's right. I'm shocked I didn't realize it myself. It would've been the end of our fourth year together. We only fell a few months short. It's the kind of length adults roll their eyes at sometimes when they think I'm being ridiculous for acting like we've been together forever, like we might be together forever. But what do they want from me? I won't even be sixteen for a few more weeks. Four years is 25 percent of my life, and that's including the parts I don't remember because I was a literal infant. Was it so wild for me to think that my first love might turn into forever? That after all that time, Ally might become a permanent fixture in my life? She turned into the foundation on which I saw the rest of high school, and, in my wildest daydreams, all the moments beyond that, too. Adult eye rolls be damned, I loved her, and I was all-in on us. Only to find out she saw me as a high school fling all along.

I think that has to earn me some internal breakup dramatics.

"I guess it would have been," I say. June 21. I can't believe I forgot.

Twyla peers at me over her phone screen, and I snap back to the moment. "And you're not supposed to be on social media."

"Right. Sorry," she says, not sounding sorry at all, as she hands her phone back to me. I lock it away, shaking my head. Twyla runs off down the dirt path that leads to the field where the rest of the camp has gathered for free play, probably to spread the good word about my anniversary.

I'm right—by the time I get to the field, Nessa and Ella are shooting me looks so saccharine, I could drown in their pity. I wave brightly at them as I make a beeline for Fitz. He's supposed to be leading an all-camp bonding activity. The entire camp is standing in a huge circle, playing some kind of memory game involving dance moves and group storytelling, but clumps of kids are starting to break off in small huddles. I flush as I realize that Ella, Nessa, and Twyla are each presiding over their own group, heads huddled in a way that screams *Juicy gossip happening here!*

I don't need two guesses to know what they're talking about.

"Let's stay in the circle," Fitz calls from the center, but not even his affable nature is enough to rescue me. One of Ben's campers is faithfully trying to recreate the high kick move the person before him came up with, but he's one of the only ones still paying attention to the game. The kids not actively part of the gossip are craning their necks, trying to figure out what's going on.

I feel trapped, helpless as Ben and Celia run around the circle, trying to get the kids to pay attention again. I want to help, but getting closer will probably only fuel their interest. Even now, on the outskirts, sideways glances float my way along with snippets of their conversations.

"It's HER? Are you sure?"

"No way she actually dated—"

"It would've been today?"

"No wonder she—"

"But Allyson Hendricks is *famous!*"

As if sensing that a disaster is unfolding for me, Rynn appears at my side.

"Wreaking more havoc?" she asks, gazing over what used to be a circle. "And without even saying a word. Impressive."

"I didn't do anything."

"I heard you dated a celebrity," Rynn says, the beginnings of a shit-eating grin at the corners of her lips. "Sort of impressive, Raines."

I glare at her. Dating Ally should be the least impressive thing about me, but everyone seems to agree with her that it's actually all I have to offer. "What do you want?"

"For you to admit that you're not cut out for the director job and let me have it," Rynn says easily.

"Absolutely not." The answer is so clear now that I hear her say it. Turning down the job means handing it to Rynn. It means giving in to the rough start I've had at being a counselor so far and giving up before I've had time to work at getting better. Worst of all, it means admitting the only thing I have to offer to this camp is fodder for the rumor mill. "I'm taking it."

And before Rynn has time to respond, I turn on my heel and march up the grassy slope to tell Ms. P the same.

IvyRaines [52 weeks ago]: happy anniversary to the first-best girlfriend and fourth-best sci fi actress out there!

I SIT BEHIND THE TABLE, MY HANDS FOLDED ON THE smooth wood, staring straight ahead. Ms. P took pity on us when the weather this afternoon cracked ninety degrees and let us hold auditions in the dance studio, so the blast of the AC sends chills where it lands on the sweaty tendrils of hair at the back of my neck. Rynn sits next to me, her hands tucked under her thighs, staring ahead just as rigidly as I am.

Turns out she was just as unwilling as I was to cede the director job. So here we are.

Collaborators.

Campers get free play and camp-wide theater games all

afternoon, run by the other counselors, while each kid takes a turn coming to the studio to perform their song of choice. So far I've sat through eight billion renditions of "Popular." The worst part is, I know Rynn hates *Wicked*. It's one of her many, many incorrect opinions. She thinks it's oversaturated, and every other kid who walks in here is proving her right. If we were still friends, we'd be cracking up about it between auditions. As it is, we can barely look at each other.

Rynn scribbles onto her clipboard as Ella leaves the room. I can tell from the way she slams the pen against the paper that it's nothing complimentary.

"You can't disqualify people just because they chose *Wicked*," I tell her, craning my neck to read what she's writing.

"And why not? Would it kill them to go deeper than Broadway's greatest hits?" Rynn says. "Or at least farther down the top-ten chart."

"*Wicked* is a classic and you just need to come around to that."

She clicks her pen shut and looks at me for the first time since we got here. "I most certainly do not. It is a perfectly fine musical objectively, but that doesn't mean it's the *only one*."

"Not everything can be all *Great Comet*, all the time." This sticks in my throat as I say it. *Great Comet* is the last show we went to see together. We spent the entire first half of sixth grade babysitting to afford seats onstage. Four months later, we weren't friends anymore.

She leans forward in her chair, agitated. "I don't see why not."

"It could be worse. They could be singing songs from *Phantom of the Opera*."

That gets her going on an Andrew Lloyd Webber rant I spent my whole childhood listening to. Turns out I inadvertently set up Sammy for failure, because he walks in ready to perform "The Music of the Night," and I can tell Rynn spends his rendition trying to bite back a laugh.

"Thank you so much," I tell Sammy when he finishes, because I can tell Rynn is going to laugh if she opens her mouth. She smiles and nods at him, waiting until the front door has safely slammed closed before she dares to make eye contact with me.

I blink at her, and then we burst into laughter. It feels good, for a moment. Giving in to the history we have so much of. I've had so many belly laughs next to this girl, meeting her crinkled eyes only to double down again.

But then she shakes her head. "I can't believe these kids. Just awful taste right and left."

"Don't be so judgy," I say with a sigh.

"I was just—" It's her turn to huff a sigh, her exasperation blowing a strand of hair off her face. "Never mind."

For a moment I feel bad. She was trying to keep the joke going, and I misread it and jumped down her throat. But then I remember the way she expected me to give this job up yesterday—the way she just completely dismissed me instead of helping me deal with the campers' gossip train—and I gotta say, that really helps ease my guilt.

Seven auditions later, including three more performances of

"Popular" and one surprise "I'm Not That Girl," we have our preliminary choices for Wendy and Peter narrowed to a top three. From there, we can't stop arguing.

"Ella would be a bananas choice," Rynn insists. "She had no comedic timing."

"Did you not hear the joke she made when she walked in?" Ella's one of the funniest kids in my group. I won't stand for this slander.

"I did not," Rynn says flatly. "Nor did I hear you laugh."

I sigh, looking down at my notes. "I think Nessa could be a great choice for Wendy. She's so sweet."

"Yeah, but she didn't check off Wendy as a role she's interested in," Rynn says, flipping back to the registration paperwork. "She's only interested in ensemble."

"Maybe she just needs a push," I say, thinking of the way she disappears behind Twyla. I wouldn't be surprised if Twyla said she was going out for Wendy, and Nessa decided that meant she wasn't going to herself.

"Maybe she just needs her boundaries respected," Rynn says.

"Maybe she just needs to be seen and appreciated for who she is," I snap back.

Rynn rolls her eyes. "Ms. P gets the final say. Let's just tell her what we think and let her choose."

"Shouldn't we at least try to present a united front?" I point out. "For professionalism's sake?"

Rynn sighs, closing her eyes as she leans back in her chair. Despite the best efforts of the AC unit, which is still working overtime in the window behind us, beads of sweat dot the sides of her forehead, and the thick straps of her purple tank top are damp. I'm sure my unwise choice of a gray cotton T-shirt is doing the most to showcase how overheated I am, but my strategy of avoiding a sideways glance in the mirror lining the wall next to us has paid off.

"We can present a united front if you agree Twyla is the obvious choice for Wendy," Rynn says, tapping her pen against her clipboard.

I stare at her. I can't help it. She just gets to me, her every word burrowing under my skin like needles tattooing her dismissiveness into me. Just because she wants theater as a career and I'm only in it for the teaching doesn't mean her opinion matters more than mine. That was always Ally's narrative, that my dreams were smaller and less important than hers, but it can't be what Rynn sees. I refuse to live through this storyline again.

At least, I hope not.

"Then I guess we can't present a united front," I say.

"Great." Rynn stands, snapping up her notes. "We can each email her our takes, and she'll take it from there."

"Fantastic. So glad we're collaborators." The words slip out before I can stop them, and I immediately regret the snark. It's that sixth grader in me, with the pettiness and waspish hurt being around Rynn brings out. As if she's a walking time portal taking me back to that moment when she said we can't be friends anymore.

Rynn just rolls her eyes at me and strides out ahead of me, letting the studio door slam behind her.

FREE PLAY IS THE MOST TUMULTUOUS TIME AT CAMP.
The field fills with the sound of yelling, coming everywhere
from the soccer game to the gaga ball pit. I hover on the edges of
the field, where the tall grasses haven't been mowed or trampled
by enthusiastic Frisbee playing. I hate to admit it, but I'm terrified of these tweens. Every time someone throws a wayward
glance my way, I want to shrivel until I'm small enough to hide
among the purple wildflowers dotting the edges of the field. It's
bad enough to walk past a group of eleven-year-olds and worry
they're judging your outfit. It's another thing entirely to know
they're judging your entire relationship history.

The realization that Ally alone comprises my entire relationship history is a sobering thought.

Rynn stands pointedly on the opposite side of the field. Between ignoring her and ignoring Twyla wandering closer to me,
I deserve a Tony for Most Unbothered Actress this year.

"Counselor Ivy, I have a question," Twyla says when she
reaches me.

I can't keep ignoring her without blatant rudeness, so I give
her my best winning smile and a response I got from my favorite
elementary school teacher. "I have an answer."

"When was the last time you talked to Allyson?" she says.
"Do you know if she's going to make it back to Earth this season?"

The last time I saw Ally, she was telling me she never wanted
to see me again. But that's hardly something I can tell Twyla.

"I, uh, I mean . . . well, I haven't talked to her in a while," I say finally. "But she's not supposed to talk about what happens on the show."

"Really?" Twyla's eyes are huge. "Not even to you? It's that secret?"

This kind of thing has always bugged me—the least interesting thing about Ally is her job, and I hate when people act like it's all she has to offer—but it's more endearing coming from a kid. I can't help but grin at her, even as the needling about Ally bugs me.

"Yeah. They made her sign an NDA and everything," I say. When Twyla looks confused, I add, "Basically a corporate pinkie promise not to tell anyone."

She giggles at this, and then, mollified by the information I've given her for now, runs off to clutch arms with Ella. I take the opportunity to scan the field for Nessa, spotting her picking wildflowers by the gaga ball pit field. It's unfortunately close to Rynn's territory, but I brave it anyway and amble toward her.

When I reach her, she's settled cross-legged in a tall patch of grass to weave the flower stems together into a white-and-purple crown. I lower myself next to her, leaning back on my palms.

"Your audition was great today," I tell her.

She smiles but doesn't take her eyes off the half-finished crown in her lap. "Thanks."

"Have you thought about being Wendy?" I ask. "I think you'd be so good in that role."

Nessa looks up at me, eyes shining for a moment, before she ducks her gaze back to her lap. Her fingers twist around the flower stems, fumbling as she tries to weave the next purple-petaled flower into the crown. "Twyla wants to be Wendy."

She says it so simply, as if that settles the matter obviously and completely. I force a look of quiet confusion on my face, but internally I punch the air. Take that, Rynn. Who knows these kids now?

"Does that mean you can't go for it?" I ask.

"Well, she's my friend."

I push her one more time. "Did she say you can't go for it?"

"No," Nessa says quickly. "I mean, I just know she'd be sad not to be Wendy. And I'd feel bad taking it from her."

I want to tell her that a true friend would support her wins, that it's okay to go after what she wants. I could even tell her that I know what it feels like to live in someone's shadow, and that even if it hurts, it's worth trying to step into your own light. But I don't want to overstep any boundaries, so I shy away from saying anything. I only nod and tell her to think about it, then leave her to finish her crown. I circle the field, smirking as I reach Rynn.

"You look pleased with yourself," Rynn says when I approach. "Lined up your next movie star date?"

I choose to be magnanimous and ignore this jibe. "I was right about Nessa. The only reason she's not going for Wendy is because Twyla wants the part."

Rynn squints at me, a stray sunray catching her eyes. It makes them glow amber. "I guess we should pass that along to Ms. P."

"I guess we should," I agree, not bothering to keep the smirk out of my tone. For the first time all summer, I've bested her at understanding these kids. Now all I have to do is keep it up.

8

CampAcornHill [48 minutes ago]: The cast list for our end-of-summer production of Peter Pan went up in our main office, and our campers stormed the gates to find out who they'll be playing. Rehearsals start this week. With a bit of extra fairy dust, we can't wait to take off on this production!

THE CROWD SHOVING AGAINST THE WALL OF THE main office echoes with shouts of the same few names.

"Angie!"

"Dylan!"

"Vanessa!"

I haven't seen the finalized cast myself. Ms. P must have sensed how willing Rynn and I were to transform the whole process into a verbal boxing ring, because she pinned the cast list up to the bulletin board the day after auditions without consulting either of us. And now the entire camp is trying to get within reading distance of a piece of A2 paper. Cue shoving.

I don't dare join the fray, but based on how many times I'm hearing Nessa's name screeched out by the kids who manage to reach the cast list, it sounds like Ms. P listened to me. It's confirmed when Twyla and Nessa reach the front of the crowd. Twyla gives a screech, and Nessa's face draws inward, a sickly pallor taking over her cheeks.

"You knew I wanted it," Twyla shouts, spittle spraying from her lips. "How could you? I thought you were my best friend."

"I—" Nessa is still staring at the cast list in shock. "I . . . I didn't! I mean, I am! I mean—"

Twyla's already storming away from her, all elbows as she jabs her way back through the crowd. She stumbles in front of me, and I throw my arm out to stop her from tripping onto the dirt path. When she lifts her head, I catch a glimpse of her red-rimmed eyes.

"You okay?" I ask. I meant to tell her to go easy on Nessa, but the flood of tears threatening to spill down her cheeks tugs at my sympathy.

She shakes her head. "Nessa completely stabbed me in the back."

"She didn't," I tell her. "She was just a great fit for the part. You were great too, just—"

"Then how come I got Mrs. Darling? And *ensemble*?" Twyla says, hiccupping. "It's not fair. I was supposed to be Wendy."

"Casting goes like that sometimes," I say lamely.

"Whatever," Twyla says, shoving past me as she blinks tears onto her lashes. I let her dash off to cry it out in the peace of privacy, deciding to check in with her again later, and scan the crowd to find Nessa. She's looking a little lost, still rooted in front of the cast list, reading and rereading her name where it appears near the top. I squeeze past two squealing girls who are clutching each other as they celebrate their joint role as the crocodile, and reach Nessa, tapping her on the shoulder.

"Congratulations," I tell her.

She meets my gaze, her wide eyes accusing. "I wasn't going for Wendy."

"Yeah," I say evenly, "but not for the right reasons."

Nessa takes this in, then shrugs. "I should go find Twyla. Explain."

I will myself to tell her more. Tell her that I know what it feels like to be stuck in the sidekick role. That she deserves her own light to grow. But doing that would mean thinking about Allyson—worse yet, telling someone else about her. And I don't want to do that. So I let Nessa slip away, ducking her head as she avoids the envious eyelines that follow her to the bathrooms.

The crush of kids abates as everyone scatters to process their casting with their friends, leaving me to take in the list myself. It nettles me. Ms. P configured a perfect mix of our ideas, mine and Rynn's, our opinions melded together. I can't tell which is more frustrating: my suggestions that were compromised away to make room for Rynn's, or the fact that, combined, our ideas have harmonized into a cast that will work well together. Angie, the energetic blur of freckles and red hair who was Rynn's choice for Peter, will balance Nessa's timid presence, and the collection of Lost Boys are sure to delight on the stage.

Fitz taps me on the shoulder, and I jump. "You scared me."

"Sorry," he says, his shit-eating grin suggesting otherwise. "We're supposed to gather the kids for lunch. And we still don't have a group name. Maybe we should make them come up with one before?"

"Good idea," I say. Hopefully Fitz's warm presence will make the whole thing go better than yesterday, and we can avoid another fiasco—and another day as the only unnamed group left at camp.

"I was thinking the Cinnamon Rolls," Fitz says as he falls into step beside me, letting me lead him to our group's meeting spot by the basketball hoop in the parking lot. "If none of the kids have come up with anything yet."

"That's perfect." I kick myself mentally. It really is good. Baking cinnamon rolls is all the kids have talked about since Fitz got us into the kitchen and they got to emerge from their singing lesson that day with sticky faces and sweetened smiles. Why couldn't I come up with something that good?

My mind is too scrambled with Ally. The memory of her rounds the coils of my brain, all my thoughts filtered through her jasmine perfume. I have to get her out of there. It's not fair. I already spent our whole relationship at her side, happily playing love interest to her main character. I'm supposed to get that brain space back now. She's supposed to be gone. That's how breakups work.

Fitz clears his throat, and I startle, realizing he's waiting for me to answer a question.

"Sorry." I meet his eyes, bright and blue. "I was . . ."

"Wallowing in breakup woes?" Fitz says. He winces when he clocks my frown. "Sorry. The kids told me."

"Something else has to happen at this camp," I say, laughing. "No, I was just . . . wallowing about something super different."

"Like how we haven't had a single snack today?" Fitz says, tossing his floppy chestnut hair as he glances back toward the main office Ms. P usually keeps stocked with snacks for the counselors. "I miss those brioche rolls we had yesterday."

"Ah, to eat gluten," I sigh.

He pats my shoulder. "Yours is a tragic life."

"It really is," I agree.

We reach the basketball hoop before any of the kids, and Fitz runs for the ball, hooting about finally getting to play. He dunks it several times and is in the middle of taking a series of bows when I point out that it's still half raised to suit the eight- and nine-year-old cohort of campers who played here this morning.

Fitz huffs as he raises it, leaving me to scan the cabins for our campers. A few of them start to gather around Fitz, cheering as he attempts to make a basket with his back to the hoop. The ball bounces off a tree that could only be described as "nearby" by someone with a generous spirit and a poor ability to judge distances. Fitz tries again, congratulating himself on his progress when this time he sends the ball flying in the right direction, making no note of the fact that it went too high and is now stuck on a cabin roof.

The kids whoop alongside him, and I watch with an easy

admiration that brims, despite my best efforts, with envy. This comes so naturally to him. I have no idea how to enter this fray.

Twyla, eyes red-rimmed and indignant, walks up the dirt path, arm in arm with Ella. Nessa trails after them, casting me a hopeless look as they reach us. Now that the whole group is assembled, I gather everyone over.

"It's just about lunchtime—"

"And thank god," Fitz adds, patting his stomach.

"But before we eat—"

"*Before?*" Fitz protests. "Unless you're about to say 'before we eat lunch, we are having appetizers,' you're wrong."

I roll my eyes at him, biting back my smile. "This was your idea."

"Past me was a cruel idiot." Fitz heaves a sigh. "But we do need a group name. Have any of y'all come up with any ideas yet?"

"How about the Lying Liars?" Twyla pipes up.

"That's not—" I cringe at the desperation that seeps into my tone, splashing my uncertainty all over my words for everyone to see.

"I didn't lie to you, I just got the part," Nessa snaps, and though her voice shakes, her words are even.

"This really isn't the purpose of this," I say.

"Oh, we don't have to be the Lying Liars, then," Twyla continues, focusing her glare on Nessa, not even glancing my way, and I watch my words wisp away as if nothing came out of my mouth but mist. "We can be the Weirdos Who Pretend to Have Boyfriends."

Pandemonium.

Twyla has unleashed chaos in its purest form, and the results are more immediate than if she'd smashed a canister of angry wasps in the middle of our circle. It spirals around us, tornadoing into a storm of voices as the group processes this news.

Ella exchanges glances with Twyla, her eyebrows flashing upward.

Sammy gasps, a high-pitched shriek of surprise that I've come to know as his trademark.

Nessa hides her face in her palms, but the bright red of her cheeks seeping through her fingers confirms the truth of Twyla's words.

Fitz looks confused.

If I didn't know how to deal with the conflict burgeoning that first morning, it's nothing compared to the helplessness I feel now. It'd be easier to shatter a soda bottle onto the concrete and then scoop each drop out of the cracked pavement and back into the broken bottle before any of it evaporated into the air.

There's no stopping this tide.

"This isn't—" I stop, take a deep breath, and force my voice to steady itself. Calmness I don't feel trips off my tongue. "We're going to lunch. Twyla. I need to see you."

The sternness in my tone shocks everyone into following my instructions. A bewildered Fitz leads the group to the dining hall, leaving me to face off with Twyla.

Talk about having no idea what to do.

Her anger is palpable, roping around her. The air around her sizzles.

Horribly, painfully, it reminds me of Rynn. Of the day our friendship ended. And I realize I know more than I give myself credit for. I know what it's like to be an eleven-year-old girl watching her friendship shatter.

But I can hardly tell Twyla that. How could I admit that I know exactly what she's feeling?

Besides, after what she just did to Nessa, she should be in some kind of trouble. Publicly embarrassing her like that for earning a good role isn't okay.

I clear my throat and tell her as much.

"But—" Twyla pauses as tears fill her eyes again. "But she lied to me. Friends don't lie."

"Friends also hear each other out when they have a disagreement," I tell her. "Instead of lashing out at each other. If you'd done that, you'd know that Nessa didn't try out for Wendy. We just thought she was the best fit for the role."

Twyla sucks at her bottom lip as she takes in my words. "So she beat me without even trying?"

"That's not . . . I just mean, you owe her an apology. You really hurt her just now. And embarrassed her in front of everyone. We have to find a way to make it right."

Twyla's shoulders slump forward, and I dare let a spark of hope light in my belly. Maybe I'm getting through to them after all. Maybe this will all work out.

"She still lied to me," Twyla says. "About having a boyfriend."

"And do you think the way you handled that was the best way to go about it?" I ask.

"Yes." Twyla's voice wobbles, but she doesn't break our eye contact.

Welp. I'm completely out of words. This conversation feels like treading water, but the waves just keep getting higher, each one threatening to crest above my head. I can't risk drowning in front of Twyla, so I dismiss her for lunch.

So much for getting through to them.

I'M READY TO BE DOWN FOR THE NIGHT AS SOON AS I shut the kids' cabin door on the sound of Ella's snores, but the group chat has other plans.

Counselors

> **Fitz:** meet at the main office?

> **Fitz:** i heard there are more snacks now

> **Fitz:** and i'm SO HUNGRY

> **Ben:** see you in 5

Celia giggles as she slips out of her bunk, tucking herself into a thick cloud of a wrap. "I'm down for a snack," she whispers to me.

I could use a break from scrolling through the Ally discourse, pressing on that particular bruise to see if it still hurts. (It does.) I shut the door quietly behind us as I follow Celia out of our cabin. The darkness of night out here is so complete. It folds around us, a comforting combination of cool air and fumbling starlight. A chorus of laughs breaks through the inky silence.

Light pours through the main office windows, though someone has had the foresight to close the lacy white curtains. Celia and I exchange grins as we hasten across the parking lot, pulling the door open to join the bubble of rowdy noise.

"Welcome to the feast," Fitz says, throwing his arms around Celia and me to guide us into the room. "We have muffins—gluten-free, don't worry, I didn't abandon you—and cookies I stole from the kitchen, some Fruit Roll-Ups I found in my bag, s'mores things, though we haven't got a fire, and a truly concerning number of gummy worms that Ben had hidden in our room."

The office is littered with candy wrappers and soda bottles; my fellow counselors are piled onto the couch and spilling onto the floor.

"It is not concerning, it's a generous donation," Ben says from where he's sprawled out on the carpet. "Know the difference."

Fitz bows to him, his hand scraping the floor. "We thank you for your contribution to today's feast and tomorrow's stomachaches."

"You're very welcome."

Rynn is curled up on the couch. She meets my eye, and I can already tell she's ready, with a firecracker lit and aimed in my direction.

"I heard your group had quite the drama today," she says.

Bang. There it goes, exploding into a shower of sparks around me.

"Wait, are you in charge of that girl who faked a boyfriend?" Celia sits up on the carpet, laughing as she takes a sip of her soda. "She's honestly an icon. My girls have been so jealous of her since day one. She wouldn't shut up about that boy!"

"Wait." Ben throws his hands up. "Not the little girl with dark hair?"

"That's the one," Fitz hoots.

"Her boyfriend isn't real?" Ben shakes his head. "I don't even know her name, and she's told me about him five times."

My skin prickles as I watch them laugh and shake their heads. "Should we be gossiping about the kids like this?"

"It's not gossip," Rynn says. At my arched eyebrow, she laughs and adds, "Okay, it is, but it's also information about the campers' social dynamics we all need to know. The drama is absolutely going to continue into tomorrow, and we can better help the kids if we know where they're coming from. The stories we know about them help us know them better."

There's some truth to this, but I'm hardly going to admit that.

"I'm just saying." I sit primly on Ben's other side, arming myself with one of the muffins. "We shouldn't laugh at them. Besides, it's nothing our group can't handle."

"The way you handled our dance lesson?" she asks.

"You won one single dance battle," I remind her.

Fitz shakes his head at me as he flops cross-legged onto the floor across from the couch. "I don't know. It was pretty bad. We're open to advice."

"*We* is doing a lot of work there," I mutter.

"Let the kids know you're on their side," Rynn says with a shrug. "If they know you trust and respect them as people, they'll trust you to help them with whatever they're going through. Just be real with them."

Be real with them. As if it's that easy.

If I were being honest with myself, I'd admit this is shockingly close to what I almost did earlier today, when I was face to face with Twyla and about to tell her that I knew what it was like to fight with a friend. That my heart knew hers, and maybe I could help her.

But call me a proud member of the Lying Liars because I do not admit that. Instead, I take an indignant bite of muffin. As if I'm going to let Rynn give me advice. That would be the same as admitting she's better at this than me. I'm not quite ready to lose this competition so thoroughly.

WE STAY UP WAY TOO LATE. WHEN RYNN IS FINISHED presiding over everyone and doling out advice as if she's been recently crowned Queen of All Camps Ever, Fitz suggests a game of truth or dare that becomes a vessel through which everyone shares their deepest secrets. Rynn confesses to worrying about directing the musical, and I bravely don't make fun of her.

It even squishes at my heart when she can't look away from

her tangled fingers as she says, "It's just my first chance to prove that I can do the thing I want to do for the rest of my life, you know?"

Which is exactly how I feel about the whole teaching thing.

Still, that doesn't mean she gets to walk all over my opinions. I chomp down on my muffin as Celia admits that she can't decide if she wants to be a professional ballerina or quit dancing entirely. Ben tells us more about his back-home breakup.

"I just didn't like the version of myself I was with him," he says. "I realized I liked myself better when I was with my friends or my family. He turned every little thing into a fight, and it brought out the worst in me."

"I'm sorry," Fitz says, his light eyes turning serious. "I can't imagine you getting hung up on the little things like that, it doesn't suit you."

He's right. Ben is the kind of affable guy who finds the good humor in everything. He's always singing with the kids at breakfast or playing soccer with them during free play, and he tells the kind of jokes that are never at anyone else's expense. He definitely doesn't belong in a relationship peppered with arguments.

"Seriously," I agree. "You don't deserve that."

"Thanks," Ben says.

It occurs to me that our situations aren't so different. Ally and I may not have gotten into a ton of arguments. In fact, we did the opposite. Bright faces and painted-on smiles to cover the disagreements bubbling under the surface.

But I know what it's like to watch yourself disappear into someone else and call it love.

I also know what it's like to let someone else see you, really see all of you, and watch them turn away. Decide they don't love you anymore.

So I let the moment slide without saying anything.

The evening closes with Ben dividing his gummy worms up among us, and we split to our respective cabins. Celia and I walk back slowly, letting the night chill cling to us as long as we can before we have to retreat to the stuffiness of the cabin.

"How's your group doing?" I ask her softly, as if to not disturb the night.

She grins. "I like them. I think it helps being paired with Ben. He's so good at the fun stuff."

"Fitz is good at that too," I say, not confessing that I've yet to be asked for so much as a pat on the head.

We reach our cabin, and instead of giving in to exhaustion, I pull out my phone. Ally hasn't posted anything new today, but when I open my camera roll, my phone helpfully informs me that it's created a slideshow of photos from my last trip to LA.

I don't have to watch it. I could just close the app, set my alarm, and go to bed. I really could do that.

I don't.

A selfie of me on the plane, one I took to send to Ally.

A shot of Ally working, doing a scene with Becca.

The two of us crowded into the frame, our cheeks pressed together, smiles huge, and am I imagining the grim resolution in Ally's eyes or is it really there?

A row of palm trees behind the diner where we went for dinner before our last conversation.

I make it four photos in before my eyes brim with tears. I miss her so much. I cling to that thought like a piece of wood bobbing in the storm-strewn wreckage that my life has become, the only thing keeping me from being pulled under by the torrent of waves each photo brings. But instead of saving me, it anchors me to the storm, trapping me there to be battered by each new wave crest. *I miss her, I miss her, I miss her.* The words knot together, clogging my throat.

If I blink, the tears will spill, so I wait until I make it out of the cabin, as quietly as I can, before letting them fall. Mercifully, I do so silently. My shoulders shake, and I wipe uselessly at my cheeks. As soon as I manage to dry them, they're wet again.

I'm so annoyed at myself, which only increases the tears as my relationship-grief cry evolves alongside my frustration cry. The relationship is over. The moment has passed. Why do I still have to be trapped in all these feelings? Why can't I just be free of them, free of *her*? Why is it that I can still remember her voice so perfectly, all the things she's ever said to me echoing in my brain in exactly the way she said them?

I love you, Ivy.

I miss you so much.

I just don't think this relationship works anymore.

But then, right when I feel ready to forget her, something in me yearns for her. I want to be free of these emotions, and at the same time, I don't want to rid myself of them. This unending, unendurable pain of missing her is all I have left of the love that used to be ours. Once it goes, nothing will remain.

So I cling to the pain as I run away from it. I resent it for staying so long past its welcome as I clutch it closer to my chest.

The result? More tears.

I've wandered past the main office, midway down the long driveway leading back to the main mountain road. It's quiet here, nothing but the wind shushing through the leaves. I run my hands across my face, drying the last of the tears, and sniffle. It's such a pathetic sound that I can't help but chuckle at it.

The worst part about breakups, I decide as I find a spot to sit on a large rock by the road, is that the one person who's causing my pain is the same person I would've, before this, turned to for anything this big. I never cried this hard before without Ally knowing about it, and now not only can I not talk to her about this, but she's actually the cause of it all.

It occurs to me that she also hasn't shed a tear over the last almost-four years without telling me. Is she thinking the same thing now, drying her tears alone somewhere in LA and wishing she could tell me about them? Or have I been wrong from the start, and has she been turning to someone else with her tears for longer than I've guessed?

I sigh into the night. I could text her. I still have that draft in my notes app waiting for me to figure out what to say. I pull out my phone, glancing over it, but *PLEASE OH GOD I'M SO SAD AND I CAN'T STOP CRYING* doesn't feel like quite the right cool, calm, collected note I wish to strike when I finally pluck up the courage to reach out to her.

But I have to reach out to *someone*. I can't stand the thought of crying alone in the woods, with no one but the wind to bear witness to everything I've carried here with me.

So I dial my sister.

Lacey answers on the first ring. She must be in her tent, nestled next to Tara in their matching blue-striped sleeping bags. For a moment an odd bitterness strikes in me like a flint, sparking a little fire of resentment. It's not fair, I tell myself. I'm the one who didn't want to go. I'm the one who said camping wasn't for me. Still, I can't help the annoyance that creeps around the image of my sisters together without me.

"Hello?" Lacey's voice is muffled. "Hello? Ivy?"

"Hi," I say, clearing my throat to unclog the tears from my tone. "How's camping?"

"Hello?" Lacey sounds so far away. "Hold on, I can—Ivy? Can you hear me now?"

"Yeah," I say. The dullness of this conversation is oddly comforting. I can hardly process the unruly emotions of losing Ally when faced with something as mundane as a poor connection. "How's it going up there?"

"Amazing," Lacey gushes. "We saw a baby bear today. From super far away, which was obviously for the best, but still. Un. Real."

If I saw a baby bear in the wild, my primary emotion would be unspeakable terror as to where its mother might be, but the story only serves to water the little envy tree that's taken root in my heart when it comes to my family.

You didn't want to go, I remind myself again. You can hardly be mad at them now.

But sisterhood doesn't always call for rational behavior. The tree only blossoms.

"That's so cool," I croak out.

"How's camp?" she asks. "It's late, is everything okay?"

It doesn't take much reading between the lines to know what she's really asking. *Are you finally ready to talk about the breakup?* But I'm tired of letting these emotions own me for today.

"So great," I gush back at her. "The kids are amazing. And I got the job directing the musical. *Peter Pan.*"

"That's so—" Her voice cuts out, coming back in spurts. "Ivy?"

"I'll let you go," I say, giving in to the awful service their campsite probably has. "I should probably get to bed anyway."

"Okay," she says, and I can hear the shoulder slump behind her words. "I'm here. Nighty night."

I laugh. "Night."

I hang up and let myself linger on the rock for a few more minutes. From a distant tree an owl hoots. I get up, trudging back to my cabin to melatonin myself to sleep.

I'm going to be exhausted tomorrow.

Int. SS Callbox Galley—Night

Artis and Milo sit at the call table, staring at the plastic rotary phone. Milo reaches out and takes Artis's hand. She squeezes his fingers just as the service light blinks on.

Artis grabs the receiver and dials.

ARTIS

Hello? Hemilia? Are you there?

[Intercut. INT: Hemilia's kitchen]

HEMILIA

Artis.

ARTIS

Thank god. Listen, I—

HEMILIA

No, you listen. There's an investigator headed your way.

ARTIS

What? How do you . . . Hemilia. You didn't.

HEMILIA

I took the job in the inspection office. I had to. It's the only way I can help keep you safe.

ARTIS

By putting yourself in danger! What if they—

HEMILIA

What if they what? Find me? Arrest me? Kill me? These are the questions I have to ask myself about YOU every. Single. Day. You can't ask me to stand by silently and do nothing. Not until you're safely home.

ARTIS

I can't believe you did this.

HEMILIA

Just be ready. They're coming.

A FIRST-REHEARSAL READING IS, BY DEFINITION, LOW stakes.

We're just sitting in a wide circle, everyone's faces buried in their highlighted binders, reading out their lines for the first time as we all familiarize ourselves with the script.

This should be easy. Fun, even.

And it would be. If not for—

"Let's pause here," Rynn says. It turns out this is her favorite phrase. "What do you think Mrs. Darling is worried about in this moment?"

Twyla looks up from her script and shoots Nessa a glance. "I bet she's wondering if Wendy is telling the truth. Maybe she's worried she can't trust Wendy."

"Well, I bet Wendy is thinking that Mrs. Darling is a total control freak who can't handle it when things aren't all about her," Nessa spits.

Rynn gives me a sideways glance. I lift my palms at her.

"I'm not the one who said to pause," I mutter.

"They're your campers," she hisses at me. "You have the relationship with them."

"Girls," I say across the circle. "Let's stay in character, okay?"

"I'm completely in character, Counselor Ivy," Twyla chirps.

I lean back, propping myself up on my palms. They dig into the soft stone flooring of the outdoor amphitheater where we'll hold our performances. We'll retreat to the studios for most of our rehearsals, but I thought it'd be nice to start things off with our end goal in mind.

Rynn disagreed and is shooting me dirty glares as she nurses a pine splinter out of her palm. "Thank you."

"I'm just glad you finally admitted you can't handle them," I say as Twyla reads her next line.

"That's not— It's your job," Rynn says, agitated enough that her voice hits a shriek, and Twyla trails off, looking up at us.

"Keep going," I tell her. "Counselor Rynn is just having a moment."

"Counselor Rynn is just having homicidal thoughts," Rynn mutters. I cheerfully ignore her.

We're shaded by the trees surrounding the wide stone seats that circle the stage, but the sun is creeping over their tops. Its first rays hit Rynn right in the eyes. She squints, adjusting her glasses, and I can feel her fuming in my direction. I beam at Twyla as she finishes her lines.

"Let's pause here," Rynn says, eyes barely open, and I resist the urge to fire her, an effort that is helped by the fact that I don't actually have the power to do so. But still. Where there's a will, there's a way.

Rynn prattles on about character motivation, and I'm ready to melt from boredom. It's not that I don't appreciate character work, but it doesn't make sense to keep everyone captive during their only free play time today to do a deep dive into Mrs. Darling's backstory. Twyla can work on that with us during her next rehearsal. This time should be about letting everyone get to know the show in the first place. We should be making it *fun*.

"Why don't we keep reading?" I ask, making a big show of checking my phone for the time. "Dinner starts in an hour."

"Exactly," Rynn says. "We have eons of time."

"Mrs. Darling is still onstage," I say flatly.

Rynn winces, and I award myself a mental point. I'm right, and she knows it.

"All the same, this is important work." She gives in to the sun, lifting a hand to shade her eyes so she can make it clear that she's narrowing them in anger at me. "We can always finish the read-through at our next rehearsal if we need to."

"We should get to the end so we can feel the full breadth of the story," I insist.

"It's *Peter Pan*." Rynn stares at me. "We all know how it ends. The ship flies. Or it would if we had the budget."

A flock of birds takes off from a nearby tree, and we're interrupted by the feathery flurry above us. I watch them, resisting the urge to roll my eyes at Rynn in front of the kids.

"The point of the first read-through is to—"

"We should be focusing—"

"Will you let me—"

"I just think—"

Ella clears her throat, her fingers timidly winding through her thick blond hair. "Are we done with rehearsal? Like, could we go play?"

"Yes."

Rynn and I both jump at the sound of Ms. P's voice. I turn slowly to see her standing halfway down the aisle, arms folded across her broad chest as she stares us down. Grateful, Ella scrambles to her feet, and the kids clamber off the stage, running through the stone rows of seating to the field for free play.

Rynn and I are left alone on the stage. I rub the back of my neck as Ms. P makes her way down to us, her footfalls heavy. Her shoes clatter against the rocky floor, a metronome that keeps rhythm with the silence. Even her steps sound angry.

"What was happening here?" she asks.

Rynn and I glance at each other. If either of us tries to say anything, the other will pounce in an attempt to defend their side. It's safest to just stay quiet.

"This collaboration won't work if you don't cooperate with each other," Ms. P says when she reaches the stage. She lowers herself onto the white stone rim, resting her elbows on her knees as she stares us down. "Arguing in front of the kids like that undermines the whole production. It's unacceptable."

I stare down at my white sneakers, chastened. She's not wrong. But what am I supposed to do when I disagree with everything Rynn does? She doesn't automatically get to be the boss here. We're supposed to be *co*directors.

Ms. P lets the silence hang over us. A nearby woodpecker takes pity on us and interrupts it with his drilling.

"Take the rest of the afternoon off," Ms. P says finally. "I'm giving you homework. Take Broccoli on his afternoon hike up Crescent Trail together and work this out. I don't want it showing up at rehearsal again. Understand?"

I pick at the side of my shoe, where the canvas of the sneaker is separating a bit from the worn rubber of the sole. A hike alone with Rynn? Sounds dangerous. At least I'll have Broccoli to protect me. What can I do but agree?

Rynn must come to the same conclusion because she nods.

"Okay," I say.

Ms. P claps her palms against her knees as she stands. "Great. Broccoli's wandering in the field, you can pick him up on your way."

And with that, she leaves us to our doom.

THE THING ABOUT CRESCENT TRAIL IS THAT IT'S STEEP. I don't know how Broccoli does it, but he's bounding ahead of us on his little doggy legs like it's nothing, his tail wagging easily as he sniffs the rocky path ahead of him. I'm struggling to hide how out of breath I am, and we're only half a mile in.

"Coming?" Rynn insists on walking several paces in front of me, her hiking boots clomping as if to announce that she's ahead, but I can tell from the huff in her tone that she's as ready for a break as I am.

My body is screaming for water, but I refuse to be the first to cave. Dehydration before dishonor.

"Just want to be here to catch you in case you fall," I call up in my most sugary tone.

Rynn spins to face me, the heel of her boot grinding against the dirt. "Or are you admiring the view?"

"It is impressive to witness you struggling to hide your exhaustion," I agree, pretending I hadn't noticed that her butt does in fact look great in those leggings. She may be the bane of my existence right now, but I'm only human.

Rynn makes a face at me. We've stopped now, the argument forcing us to a halt, so I unscrew the cap of my water bottle. Rynn opens her mouth to make a dig but elects to reach for her own instead. We drink in stony silence, a momentary ceasefire.

"Ms. P is right," she says finally, tucking her bottle back into the pocket of her leggings. "We can't be at each other's throats every rehearsal and expect to put on a decent show."

I take a few steps up to reach her, hands on my hips to air out my already tragically sweaty sides, and we continue up the trail side by side.

"Maybe we just have to take ourselves out of it," I say. "Focus on the show."

"Like how we agreed to be professionals?" Rynn asks, glancing sideways at me.

I grimace. Broccoli runs back to us, tail wagging, and drops a slobbery stick at our feet. I pick it up gingerly and toss it up the trail ahead. He runs after it, and Rynn giggles as we watch his loping gait up the path.

She forges ahead, making plain her eagerness to put as much distance between us as she can, and her feet miss the dip in the rock that would've made a good foothold. Instead, she slips down its surface, screeching as she flails through the air.

I jump forward, throwing my arms out to catch her, and we land in a thicket of wildflowers, a tangle of limbs. Our legs intertwined, her head in the crook of my elbow, my nose inches from her face.

For a moment there's a lull. We're frozen with the shock of the fall, and I feel nothing at all. Then all I can feel is the warmth of her against me, the weight of her, the softness of her skin on mine. The floral scent of her conditioner.

The bruising pain explodes over my legs, and I wince, shoving her off me. She scoffs as she pulls away, scrambling to her feet. "Get off."

"Some thanks."

She brushes the dirt off her knees. Her palms are red from

where they landed. Grass stains and flower petals cling to both of us.

"*Thanks,*" she snarls.

Broccoli brings the stick back to us. Rynn throws it this time, but he doesn't go after it, returning to sniffling in wide circles around us.

I glance at Rynn, who still has a couple of twigs stranded in her braid and a smudge of dirt along her cheek, and a giggle escapes me before I can stop it.

"What?" she asks, her lips twitching as she glances at me. "You look like you hooked up with a tree."

"Me? What about you?" I step closer to her and pull a twig out of her hair. "You've become the forest."

Rynn eyes the twig and laughs. I let the giggle return, and it blossoms into the kind of full-throated, whole-body laugh we used to do all the time as kids. It's not long before we're clutching hands, the only things keeping each other upright as we wipe the laugh tears from our eyes.

"God," Rynn says when she straightens. "Keep it together, Raines. We can't put this show on if you go wild on me."

But there's none of the bite that I've grown used to in our week of working together. She smiles as she says it, and her laugh fills her tone. It's the way I'm used to hearing her talk, as if everything she says teeters on the edge of laughter, as if her voice is always dancing.

I soften, shaking the last of the leaves out of my hair. "The show must go on."

"That it must." And with that, Rynn offers me her hand to help me over the rocky incline.

We let Broccoli lead us forward in silence. The only thing that punctures it is the occasional murmur of a flower name as Rynn points to the purple and yellow petals dotting the grassy expanse around us. I smile every time. She's always loved nature, all of it, and it brings out a reflective, poetic side of her. When she pauses to scoop up a dandelion, sighing a wish into its pappi, I roll my eyes at her, but I'm melting at the recollection of all the childhood wishes she made us do.

"Remind me of your lore?" I say, huffing out the words. She always had such specific rules for wishing.

"You have to get all the pappi off in one breath for the wish to count, but it's neutral if you don't. The dandelion would never work against you," Rynn says. "Extra points for all the ones that land somewhere they could root and a new flower could grow."

I nod as I bend over to pick one for myself. "Right."

"And I added a new one, now that we're not kids anymore," she says, her eyes still fixed on the dirt in front of her as she steps forward. "You can never use the last dandelion in a patch. Gotta leave it for a kid."

I blow into the one I picked, a half thought of Ally in my mind, but even though the seeds nestle into the dirt, where they could root and grow into next year's wishes, I'm not quite sure what I'm wishing for.

We let Broccoli's footsteps lead us, pretending to listen

intently to the birdcalls and, soon enough, the rush of the water-fall that marks the end of this trail.

"Almost there," Rynn says quietly as the whoosh of the water grows louder.

I glance at her. It'd be easy enough to reach for sarcasm here, a taunt about how openly hard I'm breathing now, but the edges of her eyes have gone soft, and the small smile tugging at the corners of her lips is the same one that exists in all my childhood memories.

It'd be easier to just let myself fall back into them.

"And thank god."

Broccoli yips in delight as we round a bend and the fast-flowing river comes into sight. We follow it for a few more min-utes. The air grows fresh with water and the sweet smell of the tall grasses that grow alongside it. We walk around a little copse of trees, and find a handful of purple flowers just starting to open their petals to the world. We round a corner, and the waterfall comes into view. It's not large, even now with the snow melted from the mountaintops, but it's pretty, tumbling into a soft rainbow as it catches the sun before disappearing into the weaving stream below.

Rynn pauses, catching her breath with her hands on her hips as she takes in the sight. "I think this is my favorite place around camp."

"Beautiful," I agree.

"More than that. It's like art." Rynn's eyes are wide behind her glasses, their lenses reflecting the waterfall. Rynn has always loved art more than anything, in all its forms. Books, music, painting, fashion, weird sculptures made out of fork tines—she loves it all. It goes deeper than that for her. She sees everything as art. The plants that have taken over her mom's little apartment balcony are art. Wildflowers, waterfalls, the way squirrels eat nuts—for Rynn, life and art have always been synonymous. It's one of my favorite things about her, and it all comes rushing back to me as I watch her take in the water. "Just look at this."

I look at her instead—really look, for the first time since I got here. She's grown so much since I knew her. I used to be taller than her, but I was on the tail end of my growth spurt when we parted ways, and it looks like she'd barely hit hers. We're not kids anymore, I realize, and the thought hardens into a lump in my throat. So much time separates us now. For the first time since I saw her at orientation, I want to know how she's filled it. But if I ask her, she might ask me in return, and then I'd have to tell her about Ally. In this place, with the rush of the water and the susurrating wind in the leaves, I don't want to invoke my heartbreak. I want to let my heartbeat join the peaceful stillness of the birdsong, and rest here with Rynn in the softness of the moment.

"It's a great place," I say instead of asking her about anything. It reminds me a bit of our childhood hideout, a little trail behind her house that we called a hike when we were kids even though it was more of a walk to a slow stream through which our dogs loved to splash. I don't dare bring it up, though.

But then, to my surprise, Rynn meets my eye, and I recognize the familiar glint of remembrance in hers.

"Do you remember our hideout?" she asks.

I blink fast to stop the lump in my throat from translating itself into full-fledged teary eyes. "Yeah. Of course. All the time."

Rynn turns to me, eyebrows raised, eyes so soft. "Really?"

I nod, not trusting my voice.

"I still go there sometimes," she admits, turning away from me to stare at the waterfall. "When I've had a bad day."

"I could have used a day or two there, after . . ." I trail off, catching myself in the act of bringing Ally into this place. I don't want her here, but there's no way Rynn won't ask about her now.

Wincing, I turn to meet her gaze. Her eyes are steady, expectant, waiting for the end of my sentence. When it doesn't come, she must see what I need from her, buried in the depths of my eyes, because instead of probing further, she shifts her gaze back to the waterfall.

"Do you remember the time Peanut Butter fell into the stream and then he tried to pretend like he meant to go in?"

I laugh at the memory. PB was truly the dorkiest of dogs. "And then he tried to bring us a rock from the bottom, but he couldn't reach it?"

"What a dummy," Rynn says fondly. She takes a few steps forward and perches herself on a damp rock wide enough to fit two people. I hover where I'm standing. I can't tell if she picked it for its size, but then she rolls her eyes and pats the spot next to her. I join her, scooting back so that we're not quite touching. Broccoli runs circles around us, sniffling at every blade of grass he can find.

"Remember the day we found the hideout?" I ask.

Rynn grins. "The day you almost got expelled, you mean?"

I shake my head, laughing at the memory. It was third grade, and Rynn and I had gotten caught planning to go to the bathroom at the same time during our respective math classes so we could skip learning about addition to catch up by the sinks. Rynn didn't care much about getting in trouble. I sobbed hysterically in the principal's office, certain that expulsion was in my immediate future, and no amount of consoling from the principal could convince me otherwise. My mom let Rynn and me go for a walk that afternoon so I could calm myself down, and that's when we stumbled on the stream we immediately claimed as our own.

"Okay, but not as good as the day you got detention for writing on the bathroom stalls," I say as Broccoli flops down between us, stretching his little doggie legs. I bury my fingers in his thick fur.

"Last time I take the fall for Rach Bresnic," Rynn mutters. "All because I had a baby gay crush on her."

"We all make mistakes," I say, patting her hand.

"Still not as embarrassing as the time you carried Hannah Risken's lunch box for her for, like, a month straight."

I blush as I laugh at the memory. "Fifth-grade me had game, okay?"

"Did fifth-grade you have dignity, though?"

"Says the fifth grader who stayed late to help Mrs. Baker tidy the classroom every Friday afternoon," I tease, and Rynn rolls her eyes. I move to scratch Broccoli behind the ears, and Rynn must've had the same idea because next thing I know our fingers are intertwined.

Time stops for a moment. Her fingers are so warm and smooth against mine, our pulses mixing at our fingertips, and when we draw our next breath, it's in unison.

But then Rynn pulls away, jerking sharply as if I'd burned her, and she blushes as she fixes her gaze on her cuticles.

"She had all the good snacks!" she says, and I smile along with her, diffusing whatever just happened.

We laugh as we sit side by side, staring out at the rush of the water and Broccoli pacing along its bank. In this little bubble of reminiscence, it's easy enough to let this water be from another time, another stream, another sound of overlapping wavelets tripping around stones in their path. It's easy, here, to let things be soft, to keep our smiles as we call to Broccoli and start making our way down the path, the waterfall at our backs.

But what happens tomorrow?

Our Favorite *Telephone Hour* Finale Fan Theories

With the show's finale only a few weeks away, we're combing the internet to find the best predictions for our favorite space rebels

Here at Geek TV, we're living for Tuesday nights. The fact that there's only three more such nights before Tuesday stops meaning *Telephone Hour* and goes back to being soccer practice and after-school tutoring breaks our hearts, but we also can't wait to find out how this story ends. What happens with the <u>lost planet</u>? Will our sweet smuggler children make it back to Earth? And what about that mysterious <u>spacelink connection</u> that keeps coming up? We've rounded up our favorite theories below!

But perhaps the juiciest fan theory is about what's going on off camera. Are the newly single Allyson Hendricks and Becca Wallis really dating? Sparks sure seemed to be flying at their latest promo interview . . .

⚹

AS IT TURNS OUT, TOMORROW MEANS FINALLY GET-ting to the end of the read-through. Rynn still insists on *pausing here,* but a playful eye roll from me is enough to keep her glancing at the clock and moving things along.

"Great job today," I say as we finally hit the end and give ourselves a round of applause. "At the next rehearsals we'll start diving deep and thinking about how to bring these scenes to life. It's going to be so much fun."

"I can't wait for all my rehearsals," Nessa says as she rises, and Rynn and I exchange glances as we both clock the way her voice flounces on the word *all.*

Twyla scoffs. "You'll need them."

"Yeah, because she has *so* many lines to memorize," Ella says.

My heart sinks, a sickly acidic feeling creeping through my chest. Since when is Ella involved in this spat?

"It's hard keeping track of so many lies," Josie says conge-nially. "Oops, sorry, I meant lines."

Ella? *Josie?* I haven't heard her string more than two words together since camp started, and now she's entering the fray?

What have I done to deserve this pain?

I glance helplessly at Rynn, but she's already disappeared

with her group, leaving me to rein in Team Twyla and Team Nessa all by myself.

Joy.

I clear my throat, and the reminder of my presence is enough to put a halt to their proceedings. Instead, they stare up at me expectantly.

"It's time for free play," I say lamely. It was one thing to deal with Twyla when she was clearly in the wrong. Now that everyone has waded into this particular gossip pool, I have no idea what to do. I can't single anyone out as the instigator, and trying to talk to all of them will just result in hearing more barbed insults tossed around. I let them loose in the field with vague instructions to give each other space. They seem to listen, at least, and scatter to different activities across the field.

My phone buzzes and I snatch at it, desperate for a momentary escape from the dumpster fire of tween gossip rapidly engulfing my life. I'm expecting another embarrassing reminder that I still have my alerts turned on for Ally's name in the news, but instead it's a text from Rynn.

A real, actual text from Rynn. No matter how many times I double take, her name is there.

I swipe it open, the corners of my lips quirking when I see it's a close-up screenshot of a baby from a Renaissance painting rolling its eyes.

Rynn Walsh: *me when these campers won't stop asking to have free play in the middle of ms zheng's lesson*

I don't know my paintings as well as she does, so I don't find a new one. This exasperated baby sums up my feelings perfectly.

me: *me when they make official gossip teams*

Fitz taps my shoulder, and I knot my fingers into my hair as I look up at him, my eyes huge as they find his.

"What are we going to do about our group?" I ask.

"I really don't know," he admits.

I groan. If even Fitz, camper whisperer, has no idea what to do next, we're completely screwed. "Twessa" drama will destroy our group from the inside out.

"Maybe ask Ms. P for help?" he suggests.

"No," I say quickly, remembering the disappointment in her eyes at rehearsal yesterday. The last thing I need is for her to know how badly I'm messing up at my regular counselor job on top of the director job. If she knows there's no part of this I'm good at, there's no way she'll ask me back next summer. And then my camp legacy will be That Counselor Who Got Dumped by a Celebrity and Did a Shit Job at Counseloring. "She has a lot going on. We'll figure it out."

"Okay," Fitz says. "But if we don't, we should tell her."

"Sure," I say. I'll just have to find a way.

My phone buzzes again, and I whisk it out to see that Rynn has sent me, in peak Rynn fashion, a Mary Oliver poem. I grin, not entirely sure why, as I pocket my phone and return to my campers.

POUR ONE OUT FOR THE DANCE STUDIO AC UNIT, THE last working AC unit on the entire campgrounds, which tragically died in the night. When Rynn and I tried to turn it on this morning, we were met with a hopeless whirring sound and a sputter of dust spitting from the filter before it lapsed into silence.

It's been a sweaty morning.

We're practicing the fight choreography today, which means a lot of running in circles. When I tell Angie and Dylan, who's playing Hook, to go again, I think Dylan starts contemplating the potential use of his prop hook as a real weapon.

"It's a billion degrees in here," Angie protests. "No more running."

I glance at Rynn, who's sheened with sweat just from demonstrating the choreography Celia taught us this morning. Wordlessly, we agree.

"How about we finish rehearsal outside?" I offer.

"With some ice cream," Rynn adds.

Dylan whoops and dashes for the door, leaving us to follow him. I snatch up the sweatshirt I dropped in a corner of the studio this morning and use it to dab at the sweat accumulating on the back of my neck. I forgot about days like this when I signed up to come back to camp.

Four strawberry ice creams later, we free Angie and Dylan to rejoin their respective afternoon classes. Rynn and I are technically supposed to do the same, but I find myself lingering on the dining hall patio where we finished our ice creams, pretending to watch the birds flit between the trees. Rynn hovers next to me, watching them too.

"Can I be honest?" she asks.

I'm instantly filled with nerves. My whole body lights up

as my thoughts tumble through the possibilities. Has she been thinking the same things as me?

"Of course," I say.

"I really don't want to go back to my group," she says, flashing me a grin. I'm flooded with relief, though it's tinged with disappointment.

"I'm sure Ms. P can handle them," I say.

"And Fitz basically does all the work for your group anyway," she teases.

I play-shove her shoulder. "He desperately needs my help."

"So that's a no on helping me make surprise cupcakes for tomorrow's rehearsal?"

"Well, I didn't say *that*."

Grinning, I follow her back into the dining hall. She pokes her head into the kitchen and gives me a thumbs-up when she finds it empty. We forage through the fridge, pulling out chocolate chips and butter.

"Where's your special flour?" she asks, her familiar teasing tone making me smile. I enforced a jokes-only rule when I was first diagnosed with celiac in first grade, and she threw her whole heart into it. If I couldn't have bread, at least I could have her laughs.

I nod to a cabinet by the pantry. "They keep it separate because they are actual angels for souls with sensitive tummies."

Rynn finds the right paper bag and pulls it onto the counter along with sugar. I track down mixing bowls, and we get to work. She melts the butter and pours it into the sugar while I sift together the flour, xanthan gum, and baking soda, a rhythm we found years ago. Falling back into it now feels like finding my way back home, to a place that smells sweet like chocolate, and knowing exactly where I belong.

"The last five years," I say.

Rynn frowns at me, confused. "Jamie is over and Jamie is gone?"

I snort. "Much as I love Jason Robert Brown, I was more thinking, like, since I last saw you. What are the highlights?"

"Oh." Rynn turns back to her whisking, cracking eggs into the bowl. "Not much is different, honestly. Except that you're gone."

I swallow thickly. This brings us dangerously close to no-go territory, the silent boundary we've constructed around the memories of the day our friendship ended and the days leading up to it. Abandon all hope, ye who venture back there.

"How are your parents?" I ask, steering the conversation away from the emotional minefield she's stumbling toward.

"Good, actually," she says. "My dad got remarried last year and my mom is setting up a gallery show for the summer."

I sigh. "Damn, I miss Mama Weiss."

"She misses you," Rynn says, shaking her head. "She still asks about you constantly."

I beam as I measure out the flour and tuck the bag back into its cabinet. Rynn's mom is a multimedia artist who taught Rynn and me to appreciate modern art and always took our notes when she did freelance children's book illustrations while we were in elementary school. She's a terrible cook but always insists on trying. She's one of my favorite people.

"How do you like your new stepmom?"

"She's sweet enough," Rynn tells me. "Here, pour the flour into—thanks. Yeah, I don't mind her. She seems terrified I'm going to hate her, so it's kinda been hard to actually get to know her."

"My stepmom is the same," I laugh. "She's so paranoid we're going to wake up one day and hate her, I swear. Even though we're so nice to her all the time. Tara even laughs at her jokes."

Rynn's eyes widen. "Tara laughs at someone else's jokes?"

Tara has always been a studious, withdrawn kid, and it used to be that Rynn was one of the only people who could reliably coax a laugh out of her.

"What about your family?" she asks. "How's postdivorce land?"

"Better than predivorce land," I say, and Rynn hums in agreement. "Both of my parents got remarried. And I have a baby half sibling. Her name is Georgianna and she's pretty cute."

Rynn looks up at me, her eyes scanning my face as if it's a book page. "That was always your worst fear."

She says it quietly, knowing she's drawing from long-ago knowledge I'd never admit to her now. But nothing used to be off-limits to us, and it feels nice—right, even—that things are that open between us again.

"It was." I nod. "But Dad doesn't, like, love her more than us, in the end."

"Of course not," Rynn says, shaking her head as she starts pouring the batter into the baking cups I set up on the baking sheet.

"And . . ." Rynn glances at me, her fingers stained with flour and chocolate. "Allyson?"

Ah. I found the limit.

"She came, she went," I say without looking up from the baking sheet, closely supervising the last dollop of batter dripping its way into its cupcakey home.

Rynn doesn't push it.

"What about you?" I ask.

Rynn shrugs. "Me what? I've always repelled romance. Is it so much to ask that someone sweep me off my feet with a choreographed musical number or some vanilla ice cream?"

"Or both?" I ask, and we finish baking while humming "Vanilla Ice Cream" from *She Loves Me*.

The only sound in the kitchen now is the beep of the oven as she sets the timer. When the cupcakes are in, she leans back against the counter, and we settle into a comfortable silence.

"I missed you," Rynn says at last.

My eyes jerk to hers. I don't bother to hide my surprise.

She grins as she takes in my expression, and shrugs. "I did. I'm glad to know what you've been doing the past few years. If I'd known that following Allyson Hendricks would've told me what you've been up to this whole time, I'd have been her number one fan."

I laugh. "Following Ally mostly means knowing what Ally is up to."

She nods, and we go back to staring down the oven timer. Maybe watched ovens do a better job of things than watched pots because, eventually, it beeps. Rynn tosses me the oven mitts, and I pull the cupcakes out.

She barely waits for them to cool before setting about dolloping frosting onto each cupcake, leaving one bald. I'm already grinning at the gesture—store-bought frosting is almost never gluten-free, a tragedy that haunts my every failed attempt at homemade frosting—when she sticks a little pink-striped candle into its top.

"Happy almost birthday," she says, sliding it toward me.

I laugh as I peel back the wrapper. "It's weeks away."

I'm a Leo, and the official baby of my grade because of it. Rynn (like all my friends) is almost a year older than me, even though we're in the same grade, a fact she loved holding over my head in elementary school.

"Camp will be over by then."

"Fair enough," I say as I turn the oven off. "Thanks."

With my back to her, the oven heat in my face, it feels safer. So I say, still facing away from her for safety, "I missed you too."

Because I did.

TeleFanHour [14 hours ago]: the season finale is TWO WEEKS away, but the twists just! keep! coming! Last night's episode completely blew my mind. What did we all think?

WaverlyWren: the only thing blowing my mind is how we still don't have proof that #BecAlly is SAILING

AFTER LIGHTS-OUT, WE FIND OURSELVES BY THE firepit tonight. We all sit too close, the sparks within spitting distance, our marshmallow sticks dangling above the flames. I'm buried in my phone, ignoring the first half of the conversation. I can't help it. Ally and that fuckface Becca did an interview that aired yesterday where I swear they're holding hands under the table. I've been zooming in on stills from the interview all afternoon. Half the internet has joined me in this venture, sleuthing through the entire cast's social media for clues.

Ally always told me not to worry about Becca. *We're just friends, Ivy. Are you saying I'm not allowed to have friends?*

I never said she wasn't allowed to have friends, for the record. Just maybe not quite so much indulging in her natural flirtatious chemistry with said friends would've been nice.

They can't be dating. There's no way. We just broke up. Ally might've been the one to end things, but that doesn't mean she doesn't need time to mourn. We were together for ages. It meant as much to her as it did to me.

Right?

"Are we allowed to do this?" Ben asks, dragging me from my own personal hell.

"Restart the campfire?" Fitz asks.

"I meant ditch our campers in their bunks without us, but now I have two things to worry about," he says with a grin.

Celia waves his concerns off. "They'll come find us if they need anything. The fire is to light their way."

Ben snorts. "A good enough explanation for me."

"May I continue?" Celia is standing at the outskirts of the fire, her arms outstretched above her head. We yelled at her to perform her last ballet solo for us, and after a round of chanting her name, she agreed.

We burst into applause, and she continues her performance, pirouetting barefoot in the grass. She finishes with a flourish, and we all clap again.

"Bravo," Fitz says, jumping up to spin her around. "Can I have the next one?"

She laughs, reaching around him to play a new song on her phone, and lets Fitz twirl her. He stumbles around the logs, and it's probably a serious credit to Celia's dancing ability that she manages not to fall face-first into the fire.

"How do I do that jumpy move?" he asks, attempting a sort of hop stretch that ends with him stubbing his toe on a log.

Celia laughs. "You want to start with a good bend in the knees to give you some buildup."

Fitz tries this and propels himself several feet in the air before landing and tripping over his feet onto his butt. "Nice."

"Let me help you," Ben says, getting up and taking Fitz's hands. "I did ballet when I was in middle school."

"Well, we can't let them have *all* the fun," Rynn says, and she reaches her hand toward me. "We can surely show them up."

"*We* can do no such thing," I say as I take her hand, letting her cool fingers interlace with mine as she leads me to the other side of the fire. "I know my limitations."

"Let me help you," Rynn says softly. She guides me through a spin, and then lets me land in her arms. We do a clumsy waltz, and I stare down at our bare feet in the grass, too nervous to meet her eyes. The firelight is warm against my skin, but her hand is warmer against my hip. I let her pull me closer and drag my eyes from her feet to her face. I meet her eyes, her brown irises alight with laughter and starlight, and the closeness of them, of seeing her and being seen by her, sends a shock through me. A current burning brighter than the flames right by us.

The song ends, plunging us into a sudden silence. We spring apart, and I keep my distance as I make my way back to my log to finish making my s'more. Fitz plops down next to me, shaking the sweat out of his hair as he spears another marshmallow.

"I love our midnight snacks, guys," he says, so earnestly that I can't help but beam at him in response. We crunch down on our graham crackers—or, in my case, melty marshmallow sandwiched between two slabs of chocolate, which is a superior s'more anyway.

"You've been quiet tonight," Ben says, his eyes mischievous as they find Rynn. "What fresh new argument will you and Ivy be treating us to this evening?"

The others laugh as I blush and Rynn rolls her eyes.

"Let me guess," Fitz says, wrapping his arm around my shoulders. "Rynn's vision for children's musical theater is morally corrupt and evil."

"You're so right," I say. "Finally, someone else sees it."

"Just because I think we should let the children have their junior production of *Into the Woods*—"

"The show is pointless without the second act! We might as well just put on Disney's *Cinderella* and call it a day!"

"They're *children*—"

"And, famously, *children will listen*—"

"How about y'all just kiss already so we can be free," Fitz says.

That stops us in our tracks. We both stare at Fitz, carefully avoiding so much as a glance toward each other. *Kiss* Rynn? Kiss *Rynn*? The thought had never occurred to me. We were just going from bitter ex-friends to ex-friends who are soft around the edges. There's no room for kissing here. Surely not.

If I look half as shocked as Rynn does, her face glowing in the moonlight as if she's been caught red-handed by a spotlight from above, I get why everyone else bursts out laughing.

To my shock, I join them. And not just because the idea of kissing Rynn is so painfully absurd that it's come full circle and become hilarious.

It's also because—

Dare I say it?

Because it doesn't sound like a half-bad idea.

FITZ POURS WATER OVER THE DYING EMBERS AS THE group disperses. Celia has gone ahead to bed, and Fitz lingers endlessly to walk by Ben. So it feels natural, normal, for me to fall into step with Rynn as we walk up the grassy slope to the cabins.

The silence as we walk is all-encompassing, but in a delicious, safe sort of way. The stars watching over us, the half moon lighting our path. I let my steps slow down, wanting to live in this moment for as long as I can. She lets her pace match mine, until we're barely moving forward, our feet wavering around the grass as we amble up the hill through the cool night air.

"Sorry about that rehearsal," Rynn says quietly, the first to break the silence. "It wasn't cool to argue with you so much, especially in front of Ms. P."

I raise an eyebrow at her, surprised. She'd been so sure she was right. But with all that softness, I have no choice—and no desire—to say anything except "I'm sorry too."

"You were right, though," Rynn says. My favorite three words to hear.

"I just . . . get nervous about being taken seriously," Rynn goes on. Her eyes downcast, the weight of her words clear on her face.

"As an artist?"

"Yeah, that," Rynn says. "In general, I guess. It feels sometimes like there's no one in my life who takes me seriously. My parents still just see me as a pawn in their postdivorce lives." Rynn's parents' custody battle loomed large over our childhoods, and it saddens but doesn't surprise me to hear that its aftereffects linger on now. "And school is . . . sort of a nightmare lately."

That stops me even in my syrup-slow steps. "Why?"

"It's just." She stops too. Swallows. Her forehead wrinkles, and the starlight itself dims when it reaches her irises. "It's so lonely there these days. I just feel sort of lost all the time. Like I can't find my place anywhere. So. I don't know. It's so embarrassing to say, but theater is a place I feel I can just *be*. So I wanted it to matter, here. And I struck totally the wrong tone. You were right."

"Wrong in the way I went about it all the same," I say. "I should've figured you had a good reason. I'm sorry it feels like that. You can keep texting me paintings when it feels lonely."

She rolls her eyes, but her smile betrays how she really feels about it. "I'll keep that front of mind."

140

We start walking again, and I let my hand swing in the space between us. Our fingers brush against each other, which could have been written off as an innocent accident, but then they intertwine.

She stops walking again, and I drift to a stop next to her. Our hands are still touching—it can't be described as holding hands, not really, but we're both flirting with the edges of each other's fingertips. My breath catches in my throat as I let her eyes meet mine.

Her eyes flicker from mine to my lips. I take a half step forward, a sudden shyness creeping into my limbs. She lifts a hand to tuck a windblown strand of hair behind my ear. Her fingers linger there much longer than they need to, and I'm moments away from letting her guide me toward her, my eyes closing, when Fitz's booming laugh catches up to us.

The sound sends a burst of adrenaline pumping through me. My eyes snap open, cheeks reddening. After that joke he made around the campfire, I can't imagine what he and Ben would say if they had seen. Moments away from—it feels strange to even admit it internally—kissing.

Rynn must be thinking the same thing because our hands fall away from each other, and when we start walking again, our pace is brisk. As if we can't wait to get to bed.

But how am I supposed to sleep after something like that?

12

AllysonHendricksOfficial [3 days ago]: And . . . that's a wrap on my time in Telephone Hour! This show has been with me since I was in eighth grade, and man have we been through some ups and downs together. I can't wait to see what's next for me, but first, time for some celebration and a huge thank-you to everyone who's loved Artis and her world as much as I have. It's been an honor playing you, space girl.

TeleFanHour: congratulations!!!! Can't wait to see the finale!

GeorgiePeach: i've been watching artis since eighth grade, basically grew up with her. I broke up with my first ever boyfriend last week and you've been such an inspiration. thank you for sharing your story with us <3

AllysonHendricksOfficial: Hugs to you. I promise it gets better.

GeorgiePeach: omg I can't believe you replied!!!!!!!!

SammyTheBadDog: WOW @GeorgiePeach you've been BLESSED

I'VE TAKEN TO HAVING JANE AUSTEN MORNINGS. THIS just means going for a walk as a hobby, but it's the only thing keeping my brain from decomposing into a pile of writhing worms. Between trying to figure out where I stand with Rynn and putting on a passable production of *Peter Pan,* all while forcing myself to participate in my least favorite hobby of Not Thinking About Ally, I personally think I deserve a medal for not imploding. Since no award ceremonies seem to be forthcoming, I settle for misty morning walks.

The camp is still quiet when I slip out of the cabin door before anyone else has stirred, rubbing the sleep out of my eyes. Despite my best efforts, I am not a morning person, and the snooze button is feeling like a great idea right now. But I know my stupid mental health needs this, so I force one foot in front of the other until I've reached the field. My mind is pulsing with last night. The memories of Rynn's hand against mine—first, sweetly, when we were dancing, and then tiptoeing around the edges of everything I haven't admitted I might want, later—overcome me.

But then, of course, that stupid Ally interview comes slithering back into the forefront of my brain, dissolving everything else into the bitterness she stirs up.

The sun is barely cresting the tops of the trees, casting a pinkish glow over the still-dewy grass. I find a tree and settle between its roots, letting the grassy morning damp seep into my pajama pants. The morning is still, all birdsong and woodpecker drilling, and I close my eyes to take a deep breath of the early air chill. Peace.

I promise it gets better.

The comment has been interrupting my search for peace since I read it three days ago. Ally almost never replies to her fans' comments. When she does, it's always benign tripe. Which I suppose this is too. But it feels like a direct attack.

I'm over you. Happier than ever. And I want to make sure the world knows it.

My eyes fly open, as if I can wake myself up from this nightmare. I suppose I could if I just stopped checking her profile. But I can't bring myself to stay away from it. If the only way I have left to keep her in my life is picking at a scab, scratch away. I want to know the story she's telling, even if I hate every word.

I'm ready to spend the next hour before breakfast feeling very sorry for myself, but the sound of nearby sniffling stops my moping in its tracks. I straighten, lifting my back off the rough bark of the tree, and scan the campgrounds. The sound is coming from the cabins, so I push myself to my feet, slap my palms together to dry out the grass stains, and follow the sniffles until I find Twyla, head buried in her knees, sitting on the stoop of our cabin.

She looks up when my shadow crosses her, tears spilling onto her cheeks. She hastily wipes her face with her sleeve, but it's wet again in moments. I don't have any tissues to offer her, so I settle for plopping myself down next to her.

"Wanna talk about it?" I ask.

She shakes her head, still focused on stemming the flow of tears.

"Fair enough." I shrug a shoulder. "I'll just hang with you for a bit then, okay?"

"Okay," Twyla says, her voice wobbling. She wavers and then lets her head fall on my shoulder as she releases a fresh round of sobs. I pat her on the back.

This is the kind of moment I have no idea what to do with. Beyond giving her a hug, how am I supposed to help her navigate the absolute minefield that is the emotional reality of being eleven years old?

"I know how hard it is," I say at last. Rynn told me to be more vulnerable with the kids, to just be real, so I may as well try that. Now that we're being nice to each other, it's easier to admit that she's better at this than me. Maybe I can learn something from her.

And I do know how hard it is. All I can think of when Twyla and Nessa argue are those last days of sixth grade. How everything Rynn and I did inflamed an argument, no matter how well we meant, until there was nothing to do but let the ever-expanding frays rip apart completely.

"Fighting with someone you love and care about is so tough," I tell her.

Twyla lifts her head, looking at me with red, dry eyes. "You mean like you and Allyson Hendricks?"

So much for being vulnerable. In the rare moments that I manage to escape the torments of my breakup story, the details just get shoved right back in my face.

"It's hard with friends, too," I say. "You and Nessa seem to really care about each other."

Twyla nods, her eyes filling again, "She's my best friend. But she hurt my feelings. I shouldn't have . . ."

But she trails off, unwilling or unprepared to confess the end of the sentence.

I rub her shoulder. "If you ever want to talk . . ."

This, I know, is a stupid thing to say. We're talking right now. I just have no idea what to say. I can't fix this issue for her; only she and Nessa can do that. And giving more advice only runs the risk of steering the conversation back toward Ally and all the heartbreak I've endured. There's only so much a girl can handle before seven in the morning.

I clear my throat. "I can help you talk to her, if you—"

"I don't want to talk to her," Twyla says, her voice hardening as if she's burned it. "She lied and I can't trust a word she says, so what's the point?"

Her cheeks have turned pink, though whether it's with anger at my suggestion or embarrassment at how much she's admitted to me, I can't tell. Either way, I let her get up and stomp back up the steps to the cabin, the door slamming loud enough behind her to wake the entire camp.

THE SUN BEATS DOWN IN A WAY THAT I FIND UNNEC-essarily aggressive as I lead the campers to the field for their post-lunch free play. Sweat beads down my neck, collecting in the hollow pool at the base of my throat. I wind my hair into the claw clip that had until now been hanging on to the pocket of my leggings. Twyla races past me, making a beeline for the gaga ball pit, clutching Ella's hand as they run side by side.

Rynn wanders by, pausing as she reaches me to take a long swig from her water bottle. "What's up with this weather?"

"You find the heat of California summer"—I pause, glancing at her with an eyebrow quirked up—"surprising?"

"You see these?" she says, pointing to the rocky mountain peaks in the distance. "We call them mountains, Raines. They cool the temperature."

I roll my eyes as I shove her shoulder, grinning as I go. I've been sweating this whole time, but a new kind of heat blushes across my face when my skin meets hers. It's enough to remind me of our almost kiss. But with the stars flushed out of view by the relentless heat of the sun, I'm less inclined to give in to the memory of that moment. The sunlight throws the choice into harsh relief, lighting up all the consequences that would be sure to come along with kissing Rynn.

But then she meets my eye, and I don't know how to stop myself from melting into the light warmth I find there.

"How's your day going?" I ask lightly. "Now that you've come to terms with the fact that California runs warm?"

She scoffs, brushing the damp tendrils of her teal hair ends off her neck. "Sweaty all the same."

As if to prove her point, she lets herself collapse into a cross-legged heap on the grass. I join her, stretching my legs in front of me, letting the grass streak my skirt with green smudges. The midday heat has come with a sort of stillness from the nature around us. The woodpeckers have ceased their pecking; no breeze shifts the leaves. The only beings around us with enough energy to move in this heat are the campers, who are somehow shrieking through it.

"I have no idea how they can do this," I say, shading my eyes to watch Nessa join some of Celia's campers in a game of handball.

"Create so much drama out of thin air?" Rynn asks.

I snort. "I meant have this much energy when it's so hot out, but that too."

"How's today been?"

"More of the same." And then I'm not really sure why I keep going. Maybe it's that, even if the harshness of the noon sunlight makes me feel like an overexposed photograph with all my flaws in high contrast, the softness of Rynn's eyes is enough to make me feel safe. At least, safe enough to spill the thoughts that have been pumping through my veins with every heartbeat all summer. "I feel so out of my depth, and it just feels like a huge neon sign that I'm not supposed to do this."

"Do what?" Rynn asks.

I wince. "Teach."

My voice comes out small. I can't help it. Ally always used to roll her eyes when I talked about wanting to be a teacher. She thought I should be going for something bigger. *I can set you up with meetings,* she would always say. *You don't have to settle. You could be an incredible writer. We could be such a power team.*

I guess she found the other half of the power couple she's always wanted to be a part of.

"You'd make an incredible teacher," Rynn says. "The way you yammer about reading and history? Any class would be lucky to have you."

I throw my arms out to the field, where my "class" of campers is scattered. "Not sure that's true."

"Oh, so the first time you ever try it, it doesn't go completely perfectly because kids have drama, and so that's a sign from the universe that the whole plan is doomed?" Rynn says, her lip quirked.

"Well, when you put it like that . . ." I shake my head at her, but I'm grinning too. "I just want to be good at this."

"You are," Rynn says, a line that sounds like a lie if ever I heard one. "Just keep asking for help when you need it. That's the only way anyone ever grows at anything."

"I tried your advice with Twyla this morning," I say. "Key word being *try,* but I think maybe it helped a bit."

"I give excellent advice," Rynn says, tossing her hair. The teal ends brush against my shoulder as they fly by. My own excessively long hair is pulled back into a thick braid that's weighing down my skull more than a little.

"True." I meet her eyes as I say it. The sunlight warms them, softening her deep brown irises, and I can't help but lean closer, yearning to melt into her. But then she blinks, and the moment dissolves into the heat of the air around us.

"What about you?" I ask, settling back onto my hands. The

grass presses into my palms. "Still dreaming your musical theater dreams?"

She wrinkles her nose, burying her freckles. "Yeah. You're the only person who knows about them now, I think."

"How?" I can't help the note of shock in my tone. "Are you saying you've found other topics of conversation?"

Baby Rynn couldn't have made it through a single conversation without tying it back to a musical or taking inspiration for her next song. I meant to tease her in a cute, fun sort of way— dare I say, a flirty sort of way—but the smile slips off her face. I lean back toward her, reaching for her with a grass-stained hand.

"Sorry," I murmur. "I didn't mean to hit a bruise."

She shrugs it off. "It's okay. I mean, you didn't, really. It's just more of what I was saying the other day, about being lonely, I guess? Like, I want to share it with people, but the thought of it is terrifying now."

Seeing the way her eyes trail on the ground, as if following an invisible bug, breaks my heart. The Rynn I knew lived with her heart on her sleeve. She never shied away from what others might think. But then, the Rynn I knew spent her childhood with her thoughts translated into custody case court documents, weaponized to fight against both of her parents. It's not hard to guess how she ended up hiding her art from the world.

"You could share it with me?" I let my fingers slide against hers, and, to my relief, she doesn't pull away. Even on such a hot day, the warmth of her skin is pleasant against mine.

Her lips wrinkle into a smile, as if against their will. "Really?"

It's strange, seeing Rynn shying away from an opportunity to be vulnerable like this. She's usually so passionate about everything life has to offer, and has been since we were little. Hiding has never been her way of being. Maybe that's why no one has noticed that there's still more that needs coaxing for her to reveal.

"I won't even make a little bit of fun of it," I say bravely, and she laughs as she reaches for her phone.

"Okay," she says, passing it to me with the screen open to the notes app. "It's not . . . I mean, it's a work in progress. Probably a bad one. I just . . . Don't . . . Well, just read it, and I guess . . ."

"Rynn." I squeeze her hand. "Chill."

She nods, inhaling sharply as I scroll through the note. It's a bit of a jumbled mess, with bullet points about plot beats and character arcs spacing out the lyrics, but I can make out the flow of the song if I squint a bit. My eyes catch on a few lines of poetry that, embarrassingly, almost make me tear up. It feels like I'm being allowed a glimpse into Rynn's soul, and I'm overcome by it.

I swallow as I reread them before handing the phone back to her. She's staring at me, her eyes huge.

"So, super chill if you hate it or think it's dumb, I pretty much think it's dumb, so, like, no pressure to enjoy, or to say anything, really, just—"

"It's great," I say, squeezing her hand one last time before letting her fingers go. "So, so good. I can't believe you wrote that. It's incredible."

She blushes, her freckles blurring into the red of her cheeks. "You really think so?"

"So much yes," I say, pointing to one of my favorite lines. "I mean, it's seriously so good. You have to show people this stuff."

She darkens her phone screen and stows it back in the pocket of her sundress, which as per usual is way too nice for a day at camp. "I don't know. Showing you is enough for now."

But there's enough wistfulness in her tone to make it clear that's not quite true.

⁂

THE DRAMA KEEPS IT UP FOR THE REST OF THE DAY. Nessa and her posse spend the day making snide remarks at Twyla's crew, who in turn bring up Nessa's romantic fakery every chance they get. This leaves me to spend the day pointlessly shushing people, only for the fire to restart every time I go back to leading rehearsal.

All in all, it's a relief to send them back to bed when the day finally, finally ends. Maybe Dad is right. Maybe teaching isn't for me.

Celia and I find the other counselors in the amphitheater, working on our Neverland set. Celia settles cross-legged on the edge of the stage, a sewing kit open next to her as she finishes mending a tear in Wendy's nightgown. I pick up a paintbrush and join Fitz, who's dotting the dried indigo streak of sky with silvery stars.

"Long day," he mutters.

I dip my brush in the silver paint and outline a small circle onto the sky. "For real."

"Are we asking Ms. P for help yet?"

I shake my head. "I think I made some progress with Twyla today. We can sort this out."

I don't mention that my attempt at progress happened this morning, before the endless onslaught of arguing that made up the rest of the day. I just can't bring myself to admit to Ms. P how badly our group is doing. My story at camp can't be one of failure. Not when failure has been the logline of my story so far this year.

"Oh good," Fitz says, and I have the grace to feel guilty.

I'm rescued from wallowing in it for too long by Rynn and Ben, who appear with a bucket of green paint.

"I was thinking," Rynn says, and then cuts off her own sentence by flicking her paint-covered brush at me, spattering my face with green. I sputter, turning to see that Ben has similarly attacked Fitz. The pair runs off, hooting.

Fitz and I only need a glance at each other before we take off after them, silver paint in hand. When we catch up to them, I dip my fingers into the bucket and then run them down Rynn's arm, startling myself with the softness of the touch. She turns to face me, her nose so close I can trace the constellations of her freckles.

I do, with fingers of silver paint, and she scream-laughs as she shoves me away, running to Ben for backup. He has a spray of silver across his left cheek, and Fitz looks all too pleased with himself, even though the tips of his hair are green.

Celia shakes her head at us from her corner of the stage, where she's been making a mess of her costume-mending duties.

"Unbelievable," she says, but she's grinning. "They'll hire any old riffraff in this place."

"You're lucky you're holding costumes," Rynn says, waving her paintbrush menacingly in the air. It sprays the stage around her feet with colorful droplets.

We retreat to our corners of the set, and I keep dotting the thin wood sky with stars. Under my new green freckles, I can feel my face heating as I think about the closeness with which I felt Rynn. Fitz's joke about us kissing comes screaming back to me, tipping me into a full-fledged blush. I'm sure I'm glowing in the night air, competing with the full moon. Is that what I want?

I glance at her. She's laughing as she teases Ben about the shape of his leaves, only giggling harder when he points out that hers look like wonky mushrooms. Her laugh that's been my home since childhood. How could this not be what I want?

But so much has happened between us since those days. It can't be as easy as a flirty paint fight and an adorable laugh lighting up the night. Nothing ever is. If there's one thing I've learned in all my years on Ally's arm, it's that.

"Can I ask you something?" Fitz asks.

"I could eat," I tell him.

"Not that," he says with a laugh. "I was actually wondering, well . . . How did you know you're gay?"

The question takes me aback, and I look up at him, startled. Then I take in his green-streaked face, the constellation Ben painted on him, and I bite back my smile.

"A lot of little moments," I say as I dab the center of a star with a dollop of silver. "A lot of crushes I didn't really recognize as crushes until this one time when a friend kissed me on the cheek—totally platonically, mind you—and I almost passed out. Never really looked back after that."

"That's it?" Fitz asks. "Having a crush? That's all it takes?"

I can't help my smile. "I mean, that's what being gay is, right? A way we love each other."

He takes his time painting the last star in the constellation we've been putting together, slowly curving his brush into a perfect circle. I take a step back to watch him.

"How did coming out go?" he asks. "If that's not too—"

"It isn't," I say softly. "It was fine. Telling my dad was easier than telling my mom, but that's true with most things. I was the first in my friend group, but they're all out now. Copycats."

Fitz snorts. "Really?"

"Yeah. My friend Emily came out as bi a few months ago, and she was the last one." I shrug. "I guess we knew each other before we knew ourselves. And that was enough to find each other."

"I love that," Fitz says.

"Me too. I love a lot of things about being a lesbian, but that's one of my favorites." I glance over at Rynn. She was the first person I came out to. Midway through sixth grade. A year before I told anyone else. When she came out to me two weeks later, we couldn't stop laughing. Two baby lesbians who'd recognized ourselves in each other. At the time, it felt like the most precious gift the universe could give me. It still does.

"Well, I think there are enough stars here," Fitz says, taking a step back to examine our handiwork.

"We did good work, McGovin," I agree.

I turn to help Rynn and Ben with the disaster plants they're creating for our forest scenery, but Fitz catches me as I move away.

"Thanks," he says, pulling me into a hug. I squish his shoulders before pulling away.

"Of course." I meet his gaze with an easy smile and, as we move to join Rynn and Ben, I can't help but wonder if we're both quietly hoping for something other than friendship.

13

CampAcornHill [13 hours ago]: Our performances of *Peter Pan* are just under two weeks away! Have you booked your ticket yet?

RESTARTING A CAMPFIRE IS HARDER THAN CELIA makes it look. Rynn is five ashy, crumpled newspapers in before she manages to get more than a few sparks to spit up onto the log. It feels like hours in the night cold before we get a small flame going.

"Good enough," Rynn says, slumping back against one of the log benches surrounding the pit. "If it goes out, I'll just quit *Peter Pan.*"

"Finally," I tease, and she purses her lips at me.

"So. Tech week."

"It's alarmingly soon." I take a seat next to her, pointing my feet at our baby fire so the little flames can do their best to warm me. "Where do you want to start?"

"With s'mores." Rynn riffles through the plastic bag she brought with her to our post-lights-out directors' meeting and hands me a roasting stick. I spear a marshmallow and let it sit above the flame.

"I think my diet this summer is concerningly gelatin-based," I say as I watch its edges turn brown.

"A critical part of any summer diet," Rynn says, nudging my shoulder playfully with hers.

We fall quiet as we busy ourselves sandwiching the toasted marshmallows between slabs of chocolate and digging in. In spite of everything that's happened over the past few weeks and the ease we've managed to rediscover between us, I feel awkward around her. There's still something in the way of our reconciliation, and here, next to this half-hearted fire of ours, might be my last chance to address it before the flurry of tech week sweeps us straight to the end of camp.

"So," I say, swallowing the last of my s'more. "We've talked about the good ol' days of our childhood. And about what's happened to us in the years since we last saw each other. What are the highlights of your life that I missed?"

"My first kiss. Emily Hart, who moved away two months later. Our new puppy, whose name is, I shit you not, Baseball. My bat mitzvah," Rynn says. "I did my service project with that animal shelter we used to walk dogs for. There were snow cones at the party. It was awesome."

"Show pictures," I say, nudging her shoulder. She fishes out her phone, scrolling for a moment before handing it to me. I swipe through photos of still-baby-faced seventh-grade Rynn: reading her Torah portion on the bimah, hugging her parents, dancing with a group of girls I recognize from elementary school, and, as promised, eating a blue-drizzled snow cone. "I'm so sorry I wasn't there."

Rynn scrolls down her camera roll to show me more pictures, ending with an art show she did at her school last year, displaying a collection of sketches of famous queer women throughout history. She zooms in on a portrait of Anne Lister to show me that the drawing's lines are actually made up of tiny calligraphed words.

"All the sketches are drawn with Emily Dickinson poems," she tells me.

I lean forward, the light of her phone screen flooding my entire field of vision. "That's so cool. And so lesbian of you."

"What are your headlines?" Rynn asks, taking her phone back.

I twist my lips as I think about the last few years. One particular headline looms large, but I'd prefer to not let Ally ruin this lovely fireside chat we're having.

"We got a dog," I say, showing Rynn pictures of Nugget, and then of Georgie when she was first born. "And that's all of it."

"Almost all of it." Rynn shoots me a sideways glance. "You still haven't told me about . . ."

"Ally? It's not like you've told me about your dating history either," I protest. "Aside from Emily Hart, of course."

Rynn looks back to the fire. It's picking up steam a bit, the flames spreading across our poorly arranged array of sticks. "Not much to report. My dating life isn't nearly as exciting as yours. Or anybody's, really. Just unrequited crushes all the way down."

"Ah." I knock my knees together. I want to ask about her crushes, but that might be picking at a scab worse than the light scarring that's formed since I bravely didn't check Ally's social media today.

"So what was the deal with you and . . . Ally?"

"It was good," I say. My eyes wander around the grass, looking at the open purple flowers and swaying dandelions—basically anywhere but at Rynn. "Until it wasn't. When *Telephone Hour* blew up . . . well, it was hard for either of us to see me as anything other than her sidekick. She was the main character, and I was her love interest. Sometimes I wonder if things would've turned out differently if she'd never auditioned for the stupid show, but when I'm being honest with myself, I think those were our roles from the beginning. She was always Ally, and I was always Ally's girlfriend."

Maybe that's not quite fair to her, to put it like that. I mean, it's not like she wrote the role for me all by herself. I went along with it. I was happy there. If she hadn't uncast me, I'd still be there, pretending I was still happy.

"That sucks," Rynn says softly. "You deserve to be in your own spotlight."

"Thanks. I guess I let it be that way because I wanted to feel loved," I admit, recoiling from my words. They're so laced with pathetic, I almost choke on them. Rynn doesn't say anything in response. She keeps her silent gaze deep in my eyes, intuiting—

correctly—that the sentence isn't over yet. That I just need a little time to reach the next part. "Because my parents . . . don't." I scrunch my nose at that, eyes screwing shut as if the confession soured against my tongue. "That's not fair. They do, I know they do. It just also feels so . . . hard for them to love me. They all fit so well together, and I'm like the easiest game of 'circle the one that doesn't belong' ever. They love me, and it'd just be easier for everyone if I wasn't part of the family at all."

"You tried telling me that," Rynn says softly. "A long time ago."

It was one of the central tenets of our last fight. We couldn't figure out how to navigate talking about our parents' divorces, how differently they unfolded, the mismatched wounds they left us with. I bite my lip. This, our last fight, is what we need to talk about, but circling around to it is terrifying. This conversation ended us before. It took Rynn away from me, and if it wasn't for this place, I'd still be without her. What if that happens again?

"I didn't do a very good job of it," I admit. It's a confession five years in the making. "I shouldn't have made it about comparing our situations."

I never did this outright, to be fair, but there was more heavy implying that Rynn was lucky both her parents wanted her enough to fight over her than I'm proud to look back on.

Rynn nods slowly. "True. But you were going through it. I should've . . . just talked to you about it when it first bugged me, instead of letting it simmer until I couldn't help but boil over."

"That would've probably been helpful," I say, smiling. "Two sixth graders who didn't have completely amazing communication skills? Unprecedented."

Rynn bursts into a laugh, and this is when I realize that she's been crying, silent tears slipping out of her eyes. In a shock of guilt, I reach out to take her hand, squeezing her cold fingers with mine.

"All the stuff with my parents left me such a people pleaser, literally tearing myself in two to make everyone around me happy," Rynn says. "I've never been great at confrontation."

I snort. "I have not found that to be the case."

"I've always been able to be more myself around you than anyone else," Rynn says without meeting my eye, so plainly it bowls me over. She looks down at our still-intertwined fingers. "Are you . . . I mean, the breakup of it all. Are you . . . over her?"

I've been asking myself the same thing all summer. I want to be, desperately. I want to be free from the shadow of Allyson Hendricks and the role we both cast me in. I want my turn to tell my own story, to define myself on my own terms rather than through someone else.

But that text draft is still sitting in my notes app, waiting to be sent. There's still a part of me that wants her.

"I don't know," I say. The excuse of trying to make Rynn feel better has passed, but there's no part of me that wants to untangle our fingers.

Maybe that's a way of being over Ally. What do I know? What does it even mean to be over someone?

"The whole 'fighting because I didn't want to miss you' thing wasn't the only thing I didn't communicate," Rynn says.

I look up at her, confused. She meets my gaze this time,

162

and there's a steely look in her eyes that sends a shock coursing through me.

"About why we fought, I mean," she clarifies. "It's that thing of pushing someone away because you're scared to lose them, you know? You were moving, and that scared me because I . . . well, I've liked you for as long as I can remember, Ivy."

I drop her hand in shock. My eyes search hers for the hint of a joke, for a trace of that laughter that lives in her irises. There's nothing there but seriousness, an earnestness I can't deny.

But it doesn't make sense.

"You said you never wanted to be my friend again."

"I meant it. I still don't."

I barely have time to react, to let the hurt hit me, before she leans in and the full meaning of her words registers.

And then she kisses me.

Her lips catch mine, and it's immediately urgent. It's as if she's awakened a need to be close to her, one that's been simmering inside me for five years and has only now been kindled into the full flame that lights me with need for her from the inside out. My body responds of its own accord before I have the time to react to what's happening. My hands slide down her sides, wrapping around the small of her back, pulling her toward me. I let her hands settle on my hips, bringing me closer to her sugary, soft lips.

Eventually, we need air. Even then we don't part all the way. I can still feel her smile against my lips.

"I've been wanting to do that for years," she said, the outline of the words forming against my smile.

"If you hadn't friend-dumped me, maybe we could've been doing this the whole time."

She shakes her head, pulling away. I pull her back, and our lips meet again before I let her speak.

"I missed you," she whispers.

"I missed you too," I say.

"Such a waste of time," she mutters.

"We'd better make up for it," I say, tipping my lips back into hers.

And we spend the rest of the evening doing just that.

Star Report: *Telephone Hour's* Allyson Hendricks and Becca Wallis

A Love Written in the Stars?

By Hannah Johnson

Teen sci-fi sensation *Telephone Hour* may be coming to an end with its third and final season, but things are just beginning for costars Allyson Hendricks and Becca Wallis. Speculation has followed the pair as they've been spotted around town in the weeks since Hendricks's recent split from her longtime girlfriend. The breakup, which came as a shock to fans who long supported Hendricks's high school sweethearts romance with ex-girlfriend Ivy Raines, was attributed to the strain the relationship faced due to long distance. Fans have been rooting for Hendricks to find new love since.

Sources close to Hendricks and Wallis, who play star-crossed lovers in *Telephone Hour,* confirm that Hendricks and Wallis are dating. "Allyson is very much in love," one source revealed. "They grew close during filming, and they're so happy together." Congratulations to the lovebirds!

TeleFanHour [3 hours ago]: BREAKING!!!! Via these grainy paparazzi pics snapped during a night out at Neon Nights, we finally have what every Telephone Hour fan has been waiting for: cold hard proof that Allyson Hendricks and Becca Wallis are more than just coworkers. They were spotted by fans canoodling in a booth. Though Artis and Hemilia may be separated on the show, Allyson and Becca are anything but!

KristenMirage: omg!!! our ship is finally sailing!

SammyTheBadDog: didn't she like, JUST break up with her girlfriend?

PaulieDavidson: ahhhh I'm so happy!! they're so cute I just can't!!!

NeonNights [5 months ago]: We're sad to announce that after eight years in the community, we'll be closing our doors for good. It's been our honor hosting your wild nights, and we thank everyone who has ever supported us.

I WAKE WITH MY LIPS STILL TINGLING. RYNN AND I didn't split to our respective cabins until way too early in the morning, the first stirring of birds already beginning over our heads as we gave in to one last goodnight kiss outside her cabin.

I don't know what this means for us. A handful of weeks ago, we hated each other. Just last week, we were barely friends. Now my lips are numb with the taste of her. Still, I don't think this can mean that we're *together* together. It's too soon. There are still things to say.

But those things will be much more fun to talk about with lots of breaks for kissing.

I roll over, my bottom bunk groaning under me as I reach for my phone. The Google Alert I have embarrassingly set for Ally's name lights up my screen with a flurry of notifications, and I smile to myself. It's time to turn off that alert. Let Ally disappear. I'm ready for that now.

And then I read too far into the first headline.

Sources confirm costars Allyson Hendricks and Becca Wallis are dating.

In a moment, I'm upright in bed, ignoring the throbbing bruise-to-be blooming on my forehead where I smashed it into the slats of the top bunk. My phone lights up my face as I take it all in unblinkingly.

167

Don't worry, Ivy. We're just friends. God, stop being so insecure. It's seriously embarrassing.

But was I insecure, Ally? I ask savagely as I crash through the Instagram algorithm, free-falling down a mess of hot takes and cooing over the happy couple. Ally and Becca. Playing two girls in love. Art imitates life. Hurrah.

My thoughts scramble into themselves. I can't make sense of this. She spent years plying me with assurances. *Don't worry about Becca, Ivy.* How many times have I heard those words, always accompanied by a verbal pat on the head?

And all the while, Becca was waiting in the wings. Until Ally was finally done with me, so the real romance could begin. The one the world's been waiting for. Or at least, the teen girl sci-fi nerd corner of the world. The news stings me with embarrassment. It's not that I want Ally back, not anymore. But I thought we were all moving past this story, letting it come to an end, and now the spotlight is back on me, spitting the secrets of my past into harsh relief. The two of them have probably stayed up late so many nights while Ally rehashes her relationship with me. I'm just a story she tells now. A story she tells to Becca. In her version I'm such a fool.

I know because I'm a fool in mine, too. Such an idiot for not reading what was plain in front of my face the whole time. Ally and Becca, all along. The entirety of my first relationship revealed to be a lie.

It takes the third pair of camper feet thudding to the floor to bring me back to my bed, my bunk in Acorn Hill, where I'm responsible for ensuring that ten children eat breakfast.

I force my phone into my pocket, run my fingers through my tangled hair. Brush my teeth. Get dressed. Go through the motions of getting ready.

The safety I felt kissing Rynn feels so far away. It was only a few short hours ago that we parted, her smile against my lips, the promise of more stolen kisses in the morning a certainty. I woke with humming anticipation, the yearning that a few kisses settled into my bones driving me to want for more, and more. I thought my moving on would mean the world would move on with me, letting this story end. But now the drama circles again, the comments section like sharks in the water around me, ready to devour this fresh news. All I want is to be done, but they'll never let me be free.

And there's still the whole day to get through.

IT'S POSSIBLE THAT CELIA SECRETLY HATES ME, BEcause she let Twyla check out her phone this morning to "call her parents." What she actually did, of course, is check all her social media, and now I'm eating grainy gluten-free pancakes while the room around me hums with the news I still haven't finished processing.

"They're seriously so cute."

"I've shipped them for ages."

"Do you think they'll get married? They better get married. Someday."

"Shh, Counselor Ivy is right there."

I blush into my tea as I chug mouthfuls of the too-hot caffeine. I'm sitting with Sammy, Arlo, and Wally this morning. Their tastes bend more to high fantasy books and sports. No talk of Allyson Hendricks's dating life here.

Rynn slides her plate of still-steaming scrambled eggs and strawberry jam–covered toast next to me, shooting me a coy grin as she settles in.

"Good morning," she says, her voice thick with flirt. "How'd you sleep?"

I swallow. It's not fair to Rynn to let everything we had dissipate into the morning air. But I can't bring myself to match her energy. I settle for a sleepy smile.

"Not enough," I say, and she winks.

Twyla and Cali, a girl from Celia's group, walk by on their way to the juice station, their heads close together. I can't decide if I want to tune in to their conversation or ignore it. I settle for taking a loud sip of tea, but it's not quite loud enough to block the next words out of Twyla's mouth from reaching my ears.

"Yeah, I mean, those pictures of them at Neon Nights were so cute."

My heart seizes in my throat. Neon Nights?

My phone is out in a flash as I google under the table, confirming what Twyla said. She's right. The pictures that surfaced of Ally and Becca, the ones that no doubt prompted the press release, are of the two of them kissing at Neon Nights. It used to be Ally's favorite club, one of the places we went out to most often when she could convince me to go out.

Key words: used to be.

Because I remember the day it closed. Vividly. We'd been walking down the sidewalk together, hands swinging between us. Our plan was to have a late lunch and loll about the park closest to her house until it was time to get ready for a night out at Neon Nights. Ally was on her phone to cover up the fact that we weren't talking—not on purpose, but because neither of us could think of anything to say. And then she gasped, letting go of my hand to clutch her phone between both palms.

"It's closed," she'd said.

"What?"

"Neon Nights."

"So we'll go tomorrow," I'd told her. I was deep in fix-it mode by that point, determined for everything that happened when I could visit her to go smoothly.

"No, forever." And then she'd shown me their Instagram post.

We'd been walking down the sidewalk together.

Key word: *together.*

Because Neon Nights shuttered before Ally and I did.

The internet has copped to this fact too. It's been posted in several comments already. *That place's been closed for months. OMG, they've been together so long! Wait, but, didn't she JUST break up with her ex?*

Which means that if Ally and Becca were photographed together at Neon Nights . . .

I don't dare follow that train of thought to the end, even though I already know where it leads. I jerk myself out of my phone, where the photo of Ally and Becca kissing in a Neon

Nights booth I know all too well is splashed across my screen, and the dining hall comes screaming back into my focus. Breakfast. The hubbub of cutlery on plates, voices overlapping, juice cups thudding against plastic-covered tables. Normal life, so far away from the closure timeline of a club in Beverly Hills.

"Are you okay?" Rynn glances at me, registering how much I'm not matching her flirty energy right now, and then glances down at my phone. Her eyes widen for a moment when she sees what I'm looking at, and then she turns back to her juice.

I lock my screen and put my phone face down on the table. "Sorry. Just. Got some news."

"So did everyone, I guess." Rynn casts her eyes across the room, realizing for the first time how many looks are being tossed my way. Everyone in the place is waiting for me to have a breakdown.

How many of them have seen the posts? How many of them know what the timeline means?

A horrifying thought occurs to me. How many of them saw it before I did? How many of these kids, these fans of Ally's, knew the truth about the real story of my relationship before me?

I grip my fork so hard, its silvery edges dig into my palm, leaving their dotted pattern imprinted on my skin. I can't bite back the fury that rises like bile in my throat, flooding my mouth with acid. I can't believe Ally put me in this position. Ending our relationship was one thing, but lying? *Cheating?*

Cheating and leaving me to find out at the same time as everyone else with Instagram and the ability to count?

Rynn must clock my anger because her hand is on my shoulder, thumb circling in soothing circles. I jerk away from it, shaking my head at her.

"We shouldn't," I whisper. The boys are long gone from our table, leaving us alone, but eyes are all over this cafeteria, and half of them are trained on me, scrutinizing me to figure out how I'm responding to this latest plot twist in my own story. The last thing I need is for everyone to think Rynn and I are dating.

"Sorry," Rynn says, glancing around. "The kids shouldn't see . . ."

"I mean, no one should, right?" I say. "Not before we really know what we're . . ."

I trail off at the surprise on Rynn's face. She blinks twice, and her eyes clear.

"Of course," she says quickly, and turns hastily back to her eggs.

I bite my lip, ignoring every instinct in me to dive back into my phone and keep scrolling until I've reached the bottom, until I've seen every angle of the story, every response, every picture, every comment, every like and reaction. As if that might be enough to give me answers.

The Brontës (if they weren't writers)

LACEY: My sunburn is NOT repeat NOT getting better

TARA: I have aloe!

TARA: Nvm it's empty

LACEY: You're dead to me

LACEY: I'm sending you all a picture so you can see JUST HOW BAD THIS IS get ready

TARA: No one wants that

LACEY: Too late

⸝⸝⸝

WITH THE SET PAINTED AND PUT UP IN FRONT OF
the copse of trees surrounding the amphitheater, our Neverland doesn't look half-bad. Our production itself, on the other
hand . . .

"Stop," Rynn calls out from where we're sitting side by side
in the first row of stone benches. "For the love of all that is good
in theater, please stop."

I shake my head at her. "They're children."

"And they're massacring everything I hold dear," Rynn says,
and all I can do is roll my eyes and bite back my smile as she
jumps onstage to show Nessa how to pretend to fly more convincingly.

When she returns to her seat, I nudge her shoulder with
mine. "You're cute when you're overly invested."

"You're simply adorable when you're so lackadaisical about
the details that it would ruin the face of theater as we know it
today if I weren't here to save it."

Rynn was always the actual theater kid among us. This camp

was my home, but I treasure these woodpecker-holed cedar trees and the smooth stone facade of this amphitheater. For Rynn, the stage is her home wherever that stage may be.

"Maybe if you weren't here being so hot it's distracting," I murmur, and Rynn turns to me, an eyebrow raised.

"Are you coming on to me, Raines?"

I lean as close to her as I dare with the principal cast a mere handful of steps away. "I thought that was obvious."

Her eyes tighten, and I know what she's not saying. I made it pretty obvious this morning that I didn't want anyone at camp to know about us. Not until we figure out what *us* means. But that doesn't mean I don't want *her*.

She swallows. "I guess we'd better wrap up this rehearsal then."

That's when a crash comes from the stage, jerking us apart as we jump to our feet. Nessa is sprawled by the front of the stage, and one of the beds is overturned. I dash to the stage, panic searing through my veins. For a moment she looks so still that all I can do is worry. But by the time I clamber onto the stage, she's getting up, dusting herself off, entirely unbothered.

"Phew," she says when I reach her, unaware of how my entire body is trembling. "This flying stuff is hard."

Then she clocks my red face and wide eyes and grins. "You thought I was really hurt?"

"I did," I confess, running through the basic first aid protocols we learned on Binder Day during orientation as I check her for signs of a concussion.

"I'm fine, I didn't even hit my head," Nessa reassures me.

"Just flopped off the bed instead of flying and completely ruined the set," Twyla snaps from where she's sitting cross-legged on the side of the stage.

I shoot Twyla my best *be quiet* glare, and nod to Rynn.

"Let's end rehearsal here for today," Rynn says, agreeing with my silent plea. "We're almost done anyway, and we'll have to fix up the set. Off to lunch with you all."

There's a hum of relief as the kids dash off through the woods to the dining hall, leaving Rynn and me to right the bed. I'm still shaky; my limbs feel like they could fall apart at the joints with how loosely they've been unscrewed.

"She's okay," Rynn says softly.

"She might not have been."

"But she is."

I nod, taking a deep breath. "She is."

"We deserve a break from all this stress." Rynn steps closer to me, taking my hand. I let her pull me into her and run her hand up my arm, where her fingers tangle into the ends of my hair. Her warmth is so intoxicating that for a moment I forget where we are.

But then the wind swooshes its way around the stage, bringing with it the distant scent of the hot dogs being served for lunch. This vegetarian/gluten-free girlie nightmare is enough of a reminder.

"We should . . ."

I take a step back, but Rynn doesn't let go of my hand. "My break is scheduled for lunchtime today."

"Mine too."

"Let's have a picnic."

I glance back at the hiking trails winding their way through the woods and grin. "Let's."

WHOEVER DECIDED HIKING IS A CUTE SUMMER DATE activity must not have sweat glands. Between the steep incline we had to scramble up halfway through this trail and the noon sun pounding on my back, I'm feeling seriously unattractive. This trail better lead somewhere *good*.

Mercifully, it does. The tight dirt path that we've been following, now dotted with a trail of my sweat drips, fans out to transform into a small grassy stretch covered with yellow wildflowers and looking out to the rich green mountain peaks and cloudless blue expanse of sky.

I let the picnic basket we borrowed from the main office fall to my feet and I follow it, collapsing onto the grass. I stretch my limbs out around me, closing my eyes as the sunrays yawn across my face. The grass rustles next to me, and soon Rynn's hand is in mine, warm as the sun pooling in my palm.

"Are you as sweaty as I am right now?" she asks.

"More." I stifle a yawn. "Definitely more."

We stay there in luxurious silence, dazed by the birdsong and the sun and the sweet-smelling grass in this slice of summer we've carved out for ourselves. Just the two of us.

"Remember the time we went on a road trip to Palm Springs? Just us and our moms?" Rynn asks.

I smile without opening my eyes, humming my agreement. Our families had gone in together on a weekend in a tiny two-bedroom condo with a community pool in the complex. Rynn and I had shared a room, and during the hottest part of the day, when even the pool offered no refreshment, we holed up in the safety of the AC and built a pillow fort, where we slept that night. Then we spent the late afternoon in the pool and dried off by the grassy stretch of lawn behind where the adults laid out with cocktails and burgeoning tans.

"This reminds me of that," Rynn says.

I let my eyes flutter open to see her propped up on one elbow, resting on her side, facing me. She grins when my gaze meets hers.

"I always missed you when you left to come here for the summer," she says, lifting a hand to run her fingers lazily through my hair. The nonchalant intimacy of the touch feels so decadent, rich with an affection I want to melt into.

"So much you started coming here yourself?" I tease.

Rynn wrinkles her nose. "Is it horribly creepy? You always spoke so highly of it here, and I love musical theater so much, and when I wanted a summer job it felt . . . nice, coming here. I wanted to tell you about it."

"But then I'd have thought you were horribly creepy," I say, and she turns away in a vain attempt to hide her blush.

I lift myself onto my elbows so I can kiss her cheek. She turns her head, catching my lips with hers, and I let her fall on top of me, her warmth flooding me with the unending bliss of summer heat.

It's much later when we sit up, pleasantly disheveled. I

finger-brush my hair, detangling the grassy, knotted evidence of midsummer making out.

"Better than Palm Springs," I murmur, pulling a strand of grass out of her hair, and she laughs.

"Should we eat something?" She nods to the basket containing our sandwiches, which lays abandoned on the grass by us.

I reach for it while she checks the time, starting when she yelps.

"We're so late."

I lean over to see her phone screen and screech so loud that a nearby woodpecker stops its work, probably to scan the area for imminent danger. But the danger is only for us. We've been up here for an hour and a half. Our kids' next classes—the ones we're supposed to be teaching—are already underway.

Grabbing the basket as I go, the two of us fly down the hill. I only take one tumble, sliding down the incline in a shower of dirt and pebbles. But I don't even stop to dust myself off. We keep running, our lungs huffing to keep up, as we dash hand in hand through the trees. My hair tangles again as it whips behind me, but even awash in panic, I can't help but laugh as I take us in: two messes clutching each other as we round the bend back to camp.

But the laugh dies soon enough, because when we're in view of the cabins, I hang back, let my hand fall out of Rynn's grasp, and try not to notice the disappointment that crosses her eyes when we enter the campgrounds with our arms hanging limply at our sides.

16

CampAcornHill [14 hours ago]: Join us on our mainstage for our production of Peter Pan next weekend! Our campers can't wait to show off all their hard work. Today, meet our directors, Ivy Raines and Rynn Walsh! Ivy is a camper turned counselor, and we're so excited to have her and Rynn at the helm of this project.

WE'RE SIX DAYS OUT FROM THE FIRST PERFORMANCE. At least everyone knows their lines.

"Theater is always a disaster during tech week," I reassure Rynn, who's developing premature gray hairs as she watches the kids struggle through the first act.

"That was . . . good," she says, fiddling with her glasses as she reaches for the compliment. "I have just a few notes. Let me—"

She hops up onto the stage and flips open her notebook,

181

pacing around the stage as she offers her ideas to the cast. I watch her with a little twinge in my gut. She might not be acting herself, but seeing her so immersed in doing what she loves reminds me of Ally. Of how much time I spent on the sidelines, watching her do her thing.

This is worse, in a way, because directing the musical is supposed to be my thing, too. My way to leave my own mark on this camp. But every time Ms. P posts about me directing the show on the camp's socials, it just reminds me about what she said during my interview. That my name could bring in audiences. Not because of me, but because of my association with Ally. Even here, that's the role I'm playing in the stories other people tell about me.

Besides, what if I get up there next to Rynn, who's been working here forever and has enough notes scribbled into that spiral journal to populate an entire novel, and say something stupid? Not saying anything is mortifying, but I feel so frozen to this ledge, my fingers gripping the rim of the seat, and I know that it's still easier than forcing myself up there and trying to compete with Rynn.

She's already won.

She bounces back to her seat for our run-through of the second act, and I smile at her. She grins back, her nose wrinkling as her whole face lights up when our eyes meet, and the self-consciousness lifts from my body. She draws an ease out of me that makes it comfortable to sit silently next to her, watching our play unfold.

At least, until we reach the climactic battle. Angie and Dylan are swinging their wooden swords around, performing the fight as we choreographed it, when a clatter echoes from the back-stage area. The action onstage stills as we all turn to listen to the shouts. They draw nearer as Nessa and Twyla stumble onto the stage.

"I can't believe you said that!"

"I can't believe you did that!"

"I didn't!" Twyla's face is red, steaming, hot with anger and embarrassment. "You're the one who lied to everyone. I would never do that."

Rynn and I exchange desperate looks. The rivalry between the girls seemed to have cooled, and now is the worst time for it to start up again.

Ella steps into the fray, standing by Nessa as she stares Twyla down, having apparently changed her mind yet again about whose side she's on. "I heard you spread the rumor about Nessa just to make her look bad because you were upset about your part."

"That's because Nessa is spreading rumors about me," Twyla shouts. She lunges for Nessa, shoving her shoulders, and Nessa tumbles backward into Angie. Rynn and I step forward, but we don't get there fast enough to stop Nessa from grabbing the wooden sword out of Angie's hand. Eyes widening, Twyla grabs Dylan's sword, and by the time Rynn and I get onto the stage, the two are yelling and smacking their play swords against each other in a decidedly un-playlike way.

I get in the middle of them, narrowly avoiding a direct hit to the face, and the girls are shocked enough that they both drop their weapons. I wasn't prepared for a lot of things that have happened at camp this summer, but a literal duel definitely tops the list. I glance at Rynn, searching her face for answers. The steeled look in her eyes steadies me. She knows what to do.

"You two need to go see Ms. P," Rynn says.

I take a deep breath, and Rynn presses her hand into my shoulder as we guide the girls offstage. I shoot her a grateful smile. Even amid onstage duels, her presence calms me.

As we walk the girls to the main office, Twyla hangs back with me while Rynn marches ahead with Nessa. Twyla looks up at me as we round the bend into the parking lot.

"Are you and Counselor Rynn dating?" she asks.

I freeze for a moment, shocked. "What?"

"You guys just seem into each other," she says with a shrug. "And obviously we all know you're single."

"I still am," I assure her. Rynn and I have not kept things as hidden as we need to. Rynn must agree because she doesn't meet my eye as we poke our heads into the main office to explain to Ms. P what's happened.

THE ENTIRE COUNSELOR TEAM WILL BE AT TOMORROW's first dress rehearsal, and I'm grateful. They've been teaching classes up until now, but with every kid involved in the production and called into rehearsal tomorrow, we'll have backup. If there's one thing I desperately need at this point, it's backup. Between trying not to think about Ally and Becca kissing, wanting to kiss Rynn and having to hide it from everyone, and the explosions that go off every time Nessa and Twyla get too close to each other, it's more than I can handle just to go to rehearsal these days, let alone run it properly.

So the five of us gather in the main office to prep for tomorrow's first dress. Rynn is the unquestioned leader, and at this point I'm happy to follow her lead. Forget leaving my mark on this place—I'll be lucky if I can make it to the end of summer without a trip to the hospital at this rate. At least I have my codirector spot. It's not everything I wanted, but it'll have to be enough.

"And then Fitz and Ben, if you don't mind hanging out backstage, I think the kids could use some support there for that time," Rynn says. "Ivy offered to come up with some theater games so it isn't completely unstructured time."

"Thanks," Ben says, and I nod.

"Thanks for running them," I tell him. I could add a joke about how much I clearly need the help, but it's already painfully obvious enough to everyone here without me pointing it out.

Besides, I'm spending all my energy on not making eye contact with Rynn. After what Twyla said this afternoon, the last thing I need is for someone else to pick up on what's going on between us. I busy myself with straightening papers, swallowing down how much I wish I could kiss her instead of doing this.

"And then Ivy and I will be out front doing notes," Rynn says without looking up from her notebook.

"Right," I agree, keeping my own focus fixed on the already-neat stack I've made. It's stilted and awful, but better to act like

I still can't stand her than to clue everyone in to how much that's changed.

"Alright, thanks, everyone," Rynn says, clicking her pen closed as she gets up from the couch. "See you all tomorrow. This should be fun. Hopefully."

I force a laugh along with everyone else. Rynn shoots me a sideways glance as we all gather our things to file out, but I dodge her gaze. I don't want everyone to see me lingering. Instead, I rush to catch up with Celia as we make our way back to our cabins.

17

AllysonHendricksOfficial [2 hours ago]: one month with my love

HenryMacson: congratulations!

JulyJulie: SO CUTE!!!!

ArlaGong: one month . . . sure

PaigetoPage: who are you to say when their relationship started?

ArlaGong: someone with basic media literacy? she's trying to cover up her cheating and I don't think it's okay.

FretaBaker: it's really none of our business

RachelWren: she's literally posting about it for us to see?

LaneyAnders: so we're canceling her over a rumor about her personal life?

FelixBants: no one is canceling! But it IS sus . . .

MY KINGDOM FOR A DAY WITHOUT DISCOURSE.

Granted, I could get this so easily if I simply logged off. But I would need more than a bit of earwax to escape the siren song of the internet. My brain is full of Ally even before I start making my way to breakfast. I didn't even seek her out this time—I muted her after the news about Becca came to light specifically to avoid seeing the cutesy anniversary posts I knew would follow, but screenshots of her latest picture and lying liar caption have been cross-shared everywhere, fueling an internet-wide fandom debate about the breakup timeline.

Her defenders are arguing that no one knows exactly when Ally dumped me, which isn't true because I remember it vividly. It was weeks after Neon Nights closed, on my next visit to LA to see her. She could've dumped me without making me drive for hours and hours, but nooooo. I made the road trip down and road-tripped right on back up to San Francisco that same night.

(It's a six-hour drive, for the eons of people following along at home.)

As I skip the line of people who can digest gluten to grab my plate of toast that looks suspiciously delicious, it occurs to me that I also have social media. One word from me would silence her defenders in a heartbeat. *I was shocked to learn from tabloids that Allyson Hendricks wasn't entirely honest with me when she dumped me and sent me packing (literally) back to SF within a half hour of me arriving . . .* The caption writes itself. Boom, canceled.

It's not like I have anything to lose. Except maybe my dignity.

I pick apart my toast without finding a table. I'm too pumped full of nervous energy to sit for a moment, so I pace by the juice station as I tuck the bread into my mouth a pinch of crumbs at a time, pretending to supervise the rowdy line forming in front of the apple juice.

My hard work is interrupted by Rynn, who taps me on the shoulder with an apologetic smile. "Hey. Can I talk to you real quick?"

She nods toward the door that leads to the back field, and I nod, suppressing a grin. A morning make-out is exactly what I need to take my mind off the doomscroll of the morning and the doomrehearsal of the afternoon. I follow her through the thick wooden door, relieved when it breezes closed behind us, blocking out the cacophony of the dining hall almost entirely.

"Where to?" I ask, scanning the field. The trouble with fields is that they're, famously, open spaces. We'll have to walk for a bit to find somewhere I can lose myself in the softness of her lips.

To my surprise, she leads me to the picnic tables that line the windows by the kitchen. We're in plain view of everyone, so I sit across from her, folding my hands on the discolored wood surface of the table, as the *we need to talk* nature of this conversation sets in, along with the sinking feeling that it's going to add to rather than take away from my laundry list of worries.

Rynn sits opposite me, fluffing her bangs rather than looking at me. "I just wanted to . . . talk."

"What's up?" I ask, but I already know. It's the same talk

I was treated to only a handful of months ago by another girl who'd decided she was done with me. Has Rynn also found someone better? Or has she just decided I'm not what she wants? That after crushing on me for all these years, the reality of me doesn't measure up?

The thoughts taste bitter, and I swallow thickly to stop myself from gagging on them.

"I just . . . don't think we want the same thing here," Rynn says, so quietly her words are almost drowned out by the birdsong carried to us on a quiet wind. "I think you're not over Ally yet, which is more than fair, and—"

"I'm so over her," I say quickly. Too quickly. Rynn silences me with a look.

"You've spent more time reading her Instagram captions than talking to me this week, and we work together," she says, ice hardening in her tone. "At least do the decent thing and don't deny it."

I run my tongue against the sharp edges of my teeth. "You have no idea how hard it's been."

"Of course I don't," Rynn snaps. "It's not like you would tell me."

"I just need time."

"Time and space." Rynn nods. "That's exactly what I'm giving you. We can't keep doing . . . whatever this is you want to do. It's not what I want. I don't want to be your secret summer fling."

"You're not . . . Forgive me for not broadcasting our one date to all our coworkers and a bunch of literal children."

"There's a difference between broadcasting it and pushing me into the plants every time someone walks by."

"I never did that," I protest, and Rynn rolls her eyes.

"It's a metaphor."

"I didn't realize you'd become a poet," I say. Rynn scoffs, turning away from me. I stare down her profile, her face glowing in the morning sun, and the urge to cry comes on so suddenly that I have to jump to my feet, desperate to be away from her before the first tears inevitably fall.

"Thanks for dumping me a second time. It feels great. See you at rehearsal, I guess," I choke out, and hasten to the rickety steps leading out the back of the dining hall before she can say anything else to me.

It's just unbelievable. Dumped twice in less than six months? By a girl I dated for years, and another who professed to be crushing on me for even longer? Have I affronted Aphrodite somehow? Is Mercury in retrograde? What did I *do* to deserve this?

Will no one ever love me enough to stay?

It's this thought that trips me from *almost crying* to *ugly-sobbing by the dumpster.* Because the increasingly obvious answer is a resounding NO. I mean, my own mother couldn't hack it. How can I expect Ally, Rynn, or anyone else to stick around when not even the woman who made me wanted to?

I have to pull myself together. Someone is bound to walk by soon, and then the whole camp will have a blast spending the rest of the day talking about how pathetic I am for losing it in public while Ally moves on with her new and improved love.

I force the tears to stop, gritting my teeth and whistling an inhale through them as I mop my eyes with the bottom of my T-shirt. Better to be wrinkled and damp than visibly teary. I don't want anyone, most of all Rynn, to know I've cried. So I stand there for a few extra minutes, leaning against the wall of the dining hall and breathing deep the scent of garbage, to let my eyes de-redden before I force myself up to gather my group for the day.

SITTING NEXT TO RYNN HAS NEVER BEEN MORE PAIN-ful. It's an actual physical pain, like wasps are building a hive around my skin every time she glances in my direction. We're sitting five seats apart, which we've silently agreed is the most distance we can manage without it translating to open hostility. She's buried in her notebook while I watch the rehearsal meticulously.

"We should tell Twyla that she should be more nurturing," I say.

"She's in your group," Rynn says without looking up from her notebook.

I guess we've tossed professionalism out the window along with any potential future kissing.

"I'll talk to her," I say, though the idea of telling Twyla she has to be sweeter with Nessa onstage only makes the wasps buzz louder in my ears. "Wouldn't want you to overextend yourself."

"I am doing everything else," Rynn says.

A warm breeze ruffles our hair as we lapse into silence,

watching the end of the first act. As soon as the Darling children are offstage, Rynn and I climb up, calling the cast back to us. Everyone crowds onto the wooden platform to sit in a semicircle around us.

"Just a few notes," Rynn says.

"Sure looks like it," I say as she flips pages and pages back in her notebook. This earns me a chuckle from a few of the kids.

"Just because I have more thoughts than you doesn't mean I have too many thoughts," Rynn says, snapping her gaze up from her notebook to meet my eyes. "Just more than one brain cell."

Twyla, still mad at me for sending her to Ms. P, oohs in response to this. I shoot her a stony look, and it actually works. She falls silent, sitting up a little straighter.

"I guess I was using my one brain cell thinking of all the things the kids did well," I say, my voice hitting an off-key octave Broccoli would be sad to hear.

"We all know you're incapable of genuine introspection and critical self-analysis—no need to announce it to the whole group," Rynn assures me.

"That's enough." Ms. P's voice flies at us from the back of the amphitheater, clear in its quiet anger.

Rynn and I turn slowly to face her, watching her stride down the side aisle to the stage.

"Celia," she says, spotting her sitting cross-legged at the edge of the stage, "would you oversee the run-through of act two?"

Celia scrambles to her feet, nodding. She shoots me a sympathetic smile as I follow Rynn and Ms. P offstage. My heartbeat is loud in my ears, and as soon as I've wiped my palms on the sides of my leggings, they're already covered in a fresh sheen of clammy sweat.

Ms. P leads us up the dirt path to the parking lot, waiting to whirl around to face us until we can no longer hear the sounds of the second act coming from the stage.

"What were you thinking?"

I can hardly defend myself here, so I stare penitently at my shoes as she keeps going.

"Fights onstage between campers are one thing, but the two counselors in charge yelling at each other midrehearsal?" She throws her hands up. "It's unheard of."

"I'm sorry," I say. Next to me, Rynn echoes my apology.

"It's clear I can't have you both running this show." Ms. P huffs. "I thought you'd be able to look past the immaturity I saw at our orientation, but I was clearly wrong. From what I understand, Rynn has been running most of it?"

I open my mouth to argue, to say something—anything—to save my job. With Ally gone and Rynn gone, it's the only thing I have left to show for this summer. But there's nothing I can say. Rynn has stepped up. She's the leader of this production. Even through the red haze of my hurt, I can still see that. Without looking at either of them, I nod.

"Great. Rynn will continue directing. You have more experience with the campers, and that's what we need right now," Ms. P says kindly, her tone softening to dull the blow of this third, final rejection. It doesn't work. All I can do is nod silently, as Rynn thanks Ms. P and turns on her heel to stalk back to the stage.

Taking with her everything I wanted for this summer.

My hands are trembling as I walk away from the amphitheater. Tears vibrate in my eyes, matching the shaky rhythm of my hands. My breaths come shallow and fast, as if I could outrun the inevitable sobfest careening my way. A first, furious tear falls on my cheek, and I swat it away. Rounding the corner of the dirt path leading to the field, I decide I'm done with crying. I'm done with hiding away, letting Ally's shadow swallow me whole. I let her eat away at me for our entire relationship, until I disappeared so much that I became easy to dispose of. And now I have no idea how to find my way back to myself.

I have to reclaim my identity. I have to take hold of my life again.

And to do that I need to take control of myself, of my side of the story. Ally's been telling the story of our breakup the same way she controlled the story of our relationship, and it's not fair. She doesn't just get to claim that and let me fall into the footnotes of her narrative.

Pausing on the dirt path in the shade of a particularly bushy pine tree, huffing for breath, I whip out my phone and swipe it open to the notes app. The draft text to Ally stares up at me. It's basically word salad at this point, after all the tinkering I've done in here. But now a new sense of clarity takes over. I feel like I finally know exactly what I need to say, exactly how to tell my side of things.

My fingers fly over the keys as I distill the entire story, from my side, into a single sentence.

Finally know the truth, and finally out from under your shadow.

My heart pounds as I reread it, a euphoric rage pumping through me.

Before I can let my brain catch up with my fingers, I hit send.

But I don't send it to Ally.

I send it to the whole internet.

18

TeleFanHour [53 minutes ago]: oh.. . . . . my.. . . . .
god.. . . . . ??? Never been so out of words

KatiePanch: I canNOT believe Ally would cheat. there's no
way. Her ex is just bitter.

AnnaSitz: no way. her post was so vulnerable and real. i
trust her

SammyTheBadDog: vulnerable?? She's SO vague we
literally don't know anything for sure

GeorgiWithAnI: speechless too . . . i always supported
their relationship so hard and seeing it come to this is
such a blow.

HannahReadsBooks: SAME. my faith in love is dead.

I SET THE INTERNET ON FIRE.

I thought it would feel good, watching the spark of my post engulf the entire fandom as its flames grew. I thought I was taking back my name. Reclaiming my story. I thought I'd feel powerful.

Instead, I just feel hollow.

Everyone's talking about it, and some of them are even on my side. They're willing to cast doubt on the perfection of their princess.

They're still renaming me in the process, though. *Her ex, her ex, her ex.* I haven't reclaimed anything. I'm still not in control. I just fanned the flames of their gossipy fun.

At least word hasn't reached camp.

Just kidding. Obviously. It's all anyone can talk about. As soon as I set foot in the dining hall for breakfast, the tables closest to me fall silent. Twyla stares at me with huge eyes, and even Sammy, who up until now seemed to have been making it through camp without hearing any part of the story, stops and stares when I pass him. I grab a slice of gluten-free toast that looks almost as sad as me and scurry to a table in the corner. I stare hard at the burnt-brown crust as Rynn walks by me on her way to the scrambled egg station. Her gait falters for a moment when she passes my lonely table, but I don't meet her eye, and she doesn't pause.

I can't blame her. In the cold morning sunlight, I'm so embarrassed of what I posted. I wish I could take it down, but it's not like it would make a difference now. It's being screenshotted and discoursed to death. Taking it down would just tell the world that I regret putting it up.

And the worst part?

Neither Ally nor Becca has posted anything in response. Their profiles are silent across the board. I thought I'd have their PR teams scrambling, but, as it turns out, I'm not even worth a response.

I float through the day. My body is completely untethered from the real world where actual humans live. It's like my whole self has been sucked into my phone, into the discourse. I can't stop refreshing every app, drowning in each fresh wave of comments. Even when I try to tuck my phone away, it's like the screen has been imprinted on the inside of my eyelids. Everything I think and do and say, all day long, is filtered through the gossip branded to the front of my brain. Even when no one's looking at me, I feel eyes pressing into my skin. It's a billion degrees out, the sweatiest day of the summer yet, but all I want is to hide under a blanket thick enough to conceal any hint of me.

No such luck, of course. Today I'm on full display.

Nowhere is that more evident than during the camp-wide improv games session we put together before dinner. Rynn is running it, flouncing around the circle in a yellow sundress that floats around her knees every time she spins. Which is often because we're playing Cross the Circle, and she's giving each group dance moves to act out and animals to portray as they make their way across the field.

No matter how hard I tried to hide behind a nearby oak tree,

199

I find myself standing in the circle. I'm in group three, and Rynn seems to be saving her most embarrassing prompts for us.

"Alright," she says. "Threes, cross the circle . . . that's made of quicksand."

Nessa immediately throws herself to the ground and starts rolling across the circle. Grass stains streak her face and clothes, but she's giggling when she gets up in her new spot, greeted with whoops and cheers from her fellow groupmates. I get away with doing an awkward leg wobble to my new place. It's all I can manage with half the campers staring at me as if I might combust and start spewing more tea about my dating history at any moment.

I should've known it would get worse than just a few stares. I should've seen the ominousness behind Ally's silence. I was too busy trying to survive the day, the stares, this game. But as soon as I reach my new spot in the circle and catch sight of Ms. P making her way toward us, her face screwed into a knot, worry blooms in my chest.

Sure enough, it's me whose shoulder she taps, me whose ear she bends to as she whispers, "Can I talk to you for a sec?"

I'm fired. So fired. It's the end. My time at camp has gone up in smoke faster than my attempt at a roasted marshmallow.

I follow Ms. P up the grassy slope. She pauses by the tallest pine tree bordering the field, and I run my hand awkwardly down its woodpecker hole–laced bark as I wait for her to fire me.

"I need to ask you a favor," Ms. P says, and I'm so surprised my finger trips into one of the tree holes. "We got a call this morning from Allyson Hendricks's representation. She wants to come here to teach a class."

"To camp?" I ask. Ally? Here? To teach?

"They said she's been doing outreach with young actors as part of the promo for a new show she's doing, and that she wants to work with local camps over the summer," she says. "There's a whole tour planned, apparently."

This sounds so blatantly fake. But then again, maybe I put her PR team in a bigger crisis than I thought.

Still, it's no coincidence that she wants to start here, where she knows I am.

Ms. P swallows. "It's not been a secret around here that you and Allyson have a . . . history. But I told you the camp is in trouble . . ."

"She can come," I say immediately. No matter how much I don't want to see her face, I know her coming here will make a difference for next year's registration. This place means too much to me to let it fizzle, and after everything I've messed up this summer, it's the least I can do.

Ms. P squeezes my hand. "Thank you."

I nod, my head broiling with too much anxiety to respond. I guess Ally's response to my post won't be coming via another internet feud. It'll happen right here, in the shade of these pines.

19

CampAcornHill [38 minutes ago]: We're so excited to welcome @AllysonHendricksOfficial to our camp today! The Telephone Hour star is coming to lead an acting workshop with our campers, and we can't wait to see what she has in store for us!

AllysonHendricksOfficial: so excited to spend the day with you! <3

IT'S A MIRACLE HER LIMO MADE IT PAST THE CURVES of the windy road that leads from the base of the mountain to the campgrounds. The parking lot is deep enough into the property that no errant photographers could have followed her, but the little black sundress she's wearing is practically dripping with camera-flash stains. Her glossy black hair is pinned up into a *look how casual and down-to-earth I am* messy bun that I'm sure took her ages to perfect. Her skin is a glowing, tanned perfection that makes my own sweaty pastiness all the more apparent. Her lips are curved into a sharp pink smile that could be an ad for the gloss she's wearing.

I wouldn't know what her eyes look like because I don't dare look right at them.

I glance over at Ms. P as Juliana, Ally's publicist, snaps a few pictures of her walking over to greet us. Ally stretches out her hand, manicured fingertips pressing into Ms. P's palm.

"I'm so glad to be here," she says, all graciousness. "Thank you for having me."

"Thank you for coming," Ms. P says. To her credit, her voice is just as smooth. She's not one to stumble over celebrity, and I'm grateful for it. "The campers are so excited to meet you."

I glance over my shoulder at the dining hall. The campers are under strict instructions to "eat something for breakfast" and "not mob our guest," but they're all pressed against the windows. Twyla's breath is fogging the glass with each exhale. I make eye contact with her, and she ducks.

I exhale through my teeth as I turn around to give them all the moment they're craning their necks to see. I meet Ally's eyes.

Making eye contact with her used to mean melting. A weak-in-the-knees, soft-in-the-heart sort of warmth that would take over my whole body. Even in our last year of dating, when we'd been together long enough for everything to grow familiar, when things between us were starting to ice over, meeting her eyes always meant melting.

Now the only thing warming me up is the beating sun,

which as per usual is doing too good of a job. When I finally look at them, her eyes are the same shade of blue: a deep, layered tone that always used to pull me in, like ocean waves. Now, looking at them too long, I'm not melting. I'm scared of drowning and I find myself yearning for the sturdier, earthier feeling of Rynn's eyes.

I blink, and the feeling dissipates.

"Hi," I say, because I've recently been crowned Queen of Embarrassingly Lame Opening Lines.

Her smile doesn't waver. "I'm glad you're here."

"Same," I say. I guess lying is just a thing I do now.

Ms. P gestures toward the auditorium. "Do you want to show our guest to the space while I gather our campers?"

I nod in one curt, stiff motion. Ms. P turns back to the dining hall, leaving me to face Ally.

"Hi, Juliana," I say, shifting around Ally to meet her publicist's eye. "Nice to see you again."

She has the decency to drop her gaze as my tone registers. Ally might be the one in charge, but she's the one who's been spinning my story to the press. I'm sure my post has made her job a living hell for the past few days, and for one vicious moment, I'm glad about it. But then it's my turn to have the decency to drop my gaze to the pavement. She's just doing her job. It's not her fault Ally cheated on me and then dumped me. It's just her job to turn that into a story that won't lose Ally her entire fandom.

"You too," she says, before gesturing to Ally with her camera. "I'm going to get a few shots of the space. Give you two some time."

I grit my teeth as she makes her way down the dirt path, sleek black heels wobbling against the errant gravel. The last thing I want is time with Ally. It was so much easier when I was just addressing a phone screen, not even thinking about the endless audience my words would reach, with no hope of a direct response from Ally herself. Now, with the depths of the ocean staring at me from her eyes, all the bravado I felt that night has sunk. I'm left hollow and ashamed.

But then I remember that she's been playing the same game. It's a game she started, in fact. That spark is enough to kindle my shame into anger.

"Shall we?" I ask in a tone that translates my words to *fuck off.* Without waiting for an answer, I start walking. I don't check over my shoulder to see if she's following. The sun is in my face, and I have to admit, it feels good for once to let her walk in my shade. "I can't believe you did all this to justify coming here."

"I wanted to talk." She shrugs. "So this is where you grew up. It's cute."

I wrinkle my nose. *Cute* has always been Ally's favorite diminutive. Clumsy fan art is *cute.* My teaching aspirations are *cute.*

"I love it here," I snap. "Look down at it all you want, this place lets kids make theater. I think that matters."

"I didn't say it doesn't matter," Ally says, her eyes widening with a practiced sort of innocence I can see right through now.

"Let's not pretend we don't know each other," I say as I yank open the auditorium door. "I know exactly what you meant."

Ally looks stunned for a moment. She freezes in place for the merest instant—the only movement the swaying of the trees behind her—before she follows me into the auditorium. She looks good even in here, under the fluorescent lights that make everyone look like total shit. Everyone except for her. Her skin glows like she brought the sunshine in with her. I used to think she had. Now I hate it.

"I can't believe what you posted," Ally says when the heavy door thuds closed behind us. "Everything you were insinuating . . . it hurt."

I stare at her. There's so much anger bubbling against my chest that it scares me. It really scares me. "Are you seriously suggesting that I have hurt you *more than you hurt me*? After everything you pulled?"

"I never did anything with the intention of hurting you," Ally says, hands on her hips as if she truly believes the moral high ground is hers right now.

I scoff, turning away from her. I can't stand the sight of her right now. The smugness oozing out of her, the sharpness of her posture.

"You got too used to a whole fandom having your back, All," I say, and my voice is ice. "You forget that I knew you before them. They never loved you like I did, and they don't know you like I do. So none of them know like I do how full of shit you are right now. Maybe I'm the last person who will ever say it to you, but it's true."

"Well, you got way too comfortable playing this little victim act to have any sense of introspection," she says.

"You're the actress," I fire back. "Seems like the last year of our relationship was your best performance yet."

Her comeback, which I'm sure was dumb anyway, is interrupted by the wheeze of the door opening. Ms. P sticks her head in, the whole camp craning their necks behind her to catch a glimpse of the screaming match. The pink in her cheeks makes it clear that our voices have carried all too well to outside ears.

"Are you ready for us?"

"Yes," Ally says, so smoothly that I stumble. She's disappeared behind that sleek mask of professionalism. All signs of her anger have disappeared, and she stands straighter as the campers file in. Next to her I look as disheveled, as beaten, as I feel.

Rynn leads her campers into the auditorium with her group, pointedly not meeting my gaze as she looks back to count them unnecessarily. I shrink away from her, desperate to melt into my surroundings. Of course, this impossible wish has never been more impossible. Everyone else is darting their gaze toward me every few seconds. The only moments they're not looking at me, they're looking at Ally.

Blinking fast to swallow past the lump swelling in my throat, I find my way to Fitz and my group. His warm and steadying hand finds mine, and the firm friendship of his palm against mine reminds me to take a breath. I meet his warm blue eyes gratefully, and his lips curve into a soft smile. For a moment I feel like I can get through this.

The feeling disappears as soon as I accidentally make eye contact with Rynn. There's nothing but accusation in her gaze, and I know that she's thinking she was right. That I'm not over Ally or this breakup, not ready to be with her.

The worst part is, after the screaming she just overheard, I can't blame her.

⚶

ALLY SPENDS THE REST OF THE DAY TEACHING AN acting class to each group, and I spend the rest of the day wondering if I could use these pine trees to build a slingshot big enough to catapult myself into the sun. My group is slated to go last, which means I have the whole day to come up with an excuse to not participate, and yet when four o'clock rolls around, I find myself trudging up the steps to the dance studio with nothing to show for my hours of effort.

Fitz bounces up ahead of me to the door, which he holds open for the campers as they shove and squeal their way into the room. Rynn's group babbles excitedly as they squish their way out, the doorway bulging as both groups insist on cramming themselves through at the same time. I find myself slowing my steps as I pass Rynn, and I realize that I'm desperate for her. I meet her eyes, and the honeyed center of her irises soften as she offers me a small smile. I open my mouth to say something—I'm not sure what yet, but I know I need to plead with her, beg her to forget this breakup and take me away from the horrors waiting for me in the dance studio.

But then she keeps walking, following her group to their next activity, and it strikes me for the first time how unfair I've been to her. It feels like the entire summer has been boiled down to the few seconds of eye contact in a warm breeze on this staircase, a microcosm of what I've been putting her through for our entire time here. I've looked to her to save me from my feelings about this breakup. Instead of going through them myself, I tried to skip over them, using Rynn to vault over the chasm of my own broken heart.

No wonder she broke up with me. She was right to break up with me. The realization lands heavy in my chest. Her dumping me is nothing like my breakup with Ally. It tears a whole new kind of hurt through me, a wound salted with guilt and shame. I can't believe I got a second chance with Rynn and I blew it on using her as a Band-Aid.

So it's with full knowledge of my own dumbassery that I walk into the studio, letting the door shut stiffly behind me, entombing me in this Ally-filled room. Awash with late-afternoon sunlight, she still shines like the brightest thing in the room. Years of certainty that all eyes are on her have given her an unseemly confidence, making it a self-fulfilling prophecy at this point: where Ally goes, eyes follow.

Except mine. Even though mine were the first to find her with the kind of admiration she's become used to, I've forgotten how to appreciate the glow of her skin. I know exactly how deep it runs, and I'm not interested in the shallowness of her light.

I tell Fitz I need a bathroom break, and I don't go back to the dance studio until it's time to pick up the kids.

I STARE INTO THE CRACKLING FLAMES LICKING THE stone-lined edge of the firepit. It's all I can do not to throw my phone into the white heart of the fire. At this point, I'll take anything to escape the tyranny of the internet, the inescapability of the hot takes, the steady stream of updates about how well Ally is doing. New love, heartbreak all but forgotten. If she was ever heartbroken in the first place. Maybe losing me was just a blip, a bump in the road on the way to her perfect life. After today, it certainly seems that way. She was all too happy to yell at me for posting something that undermined her relationship with no care whatsoever for the hurt it caused me. If she ever gave a shit about me, that's disappeared.

Everyone else has gone to bed early. It's an uncharacteristic move for our counselor group, but between dress rehearsals and tween drama—not to mention my own drama—everyone's exhausted. I am, too, but the cabin walls felt like they were closing in on me.

The night air is cold, but the dark is comforting, and it's easy to inhale in the rich night air. I wrapped myself in a wool sweater that swallows my frame completely. The fire spits sparks at the soles of my feet, falling just short. I close my eyes, wrapping my fingers tighter around the mug of hot chocolate I made in the main office before heading down here. All the hallmarks of comfort, but none of them are enough to soothe the ache that's dulled into a bruise that can't heal because someone keeps poking it. That someone being me. Well, me and everyone with internet access.

Footsteps rustle the grass behind me, and I turn to see Fitz making his way to the fire. He grins when he sees me, but it's forced.

"I see someone had the same idea," he says as he plops next

to me, extending his fingers to let the fire warm them. "You had a rough day."

"Which part are you talking about? Getting fired? My ex showing up at my job? My—" I cut myself off before I accidentally add Rynn dumping me to my list of grievances.

Fitz nods. "All of it, really. I can't imagine going through a breakup with everyone watching. Breaking up with my girlfriend freshman year and dealing with my high school class getting the news was rough enough."

"It might be the same, really," I murmur. "Just more people in on it. Sorry I ditched you during her class."

He shakes his head. "I was glad you did. You don't deserve to sit through that."

We're quiet for a moment, the fire's crackle the only sound. I glance at Fitz, watching the flames highlight the shadows on his face.

"What brings you out to stare pensively into a fire at this late hour?" I ask him.

He swallows, his Adam's apple bobbing. "Can I tell you something?"

"Of course." I sit up straighter.

"I think I might be bi?" he says, so quietly the fire almost swallows his words.

I scoot closer to him and tentatively touch his shoulder. "Dude. That's so cool. Thanks for telling me."

It doesn't quite explain the pensive fire staring, but I generously give him a few more minutes of silence before I add, "So, that Ben, huh?"

Fitz laughs, an adorable blush coloring his cheeks. "Is it really as obvious as you and Rynn?"

It's my turn to gasp. "What? Me and who? We're not—"

"It's a good thing you're a director and not an actor," he says, shaking his head. "That was the most high-pitched lie I've ever heard."

I drop my face into my palms. "I really thought I was doing such a good job."

"My dude, we all saw you holding hands when you came back from that hike," Fitz says, shaking his head. "Even if we hadn't, it's not like the tension was exactly *hidden*."

I want to dig a hole under this log so deep it'll take me back in time, to when I had never dated anyone at all and I was still very worried about my science grade. Sadly, science has yet to discover dirt wormholes, and given the aforementioned grades I used to get, I'm hardly next in line to make a breakthrough. I settle for screwing my eyes shut and lifting my face to the sky, as if sending a beacon to any aliens hoping to abduct someone tonight.

"It's cute," Fitz says.

"So are you and Ben," I say, opening my eyes. There are so many stars above us. It feels like I can see the whole universe unfolding in front of me, woodpecker holes and pines and starlight all the way up.

"You think?" Fitz asks, so earnestly it breaks my heart.

"Yeah," I assure him. "He lights up every time you go over to him."

Fitz's smile is giddy. "I can't believe I'm actually saying this stuff out loud. I mean, I've noticed boys before, you know? Maybe something about being away from home makes it easier to let myself be new, in a way."

"That makes sense."

"What about you?" Fitz glances my way. "Any newness for you?"

"How do you mean?" I ask, turning back to the fire.

Fitz laughs. "You're basically one big enigma. Ever since the beginning, you never told us anything. Even hiding Rynn! The only reason I know anything about you is because TMZ keeps broadcasting your business online. And, well, you yelled about it pretty loudly earlier."

I freeze, painfully aware of the awkwardness of my own silence. But just like I only gave Fitz a handful of minutes before bringing up Ben, he nudges my shoulder before I can slip too far into the wallow of the quiet.

"Seriously, how are you doing?" he asks softly.

"Not great," I admit, and when he hums in sympathy, it's like a little piece of my heart comes unstitched, like the wound is scabbing over and doesn't need thread to keep it together anymore. He waits long enough that I know he expects me to say more, and this time I do. "I just don't know how I'm supposed to get over someone who's all over my feed with how quickly she's moving on to better things. And better people."

"What makes . . . Becca?" I nod, and Fitz continues, a note of genuine surprise in his voice. "What makes Becca better?"

"She's . . . also an actress," I say lamely, surprised at how hard it is to come up with evidence for something I've just . . . believed. Not just about Becca, but Ally too. Destined for bigger things than me, her future written in the stars while mine was always uncertain but certainly smaller than hers.

"Do you really think they're better than the rest of us?" Fitz asks. When he puts it like that, there's nothing I can do but shake my head.

"I guess not." I smile smally at the thought. Because he's right, and with the distance he's giving me from the capital-I Industry, it's so easy to see it.

Fitz nods. "You matter to the people around you. Me, Rynn, the kids . . . this summer wouldn't have been the same without you. You're important."

It's everything I've needed to hear, and all I can do is pull him into a hug. "That means a lot."

"It's all true."

I pull away, and he grins. "Cool. We should talk more, Raines. But right now I need to go to bed. Or find a crunchy leaf."

Seeing my confused look, he shrugs as he stands. "There are, like, no trees in my neighborhood in LA. My chances to step on crunchy leaves are limited, and I hear it's delightful."

"Good luck with that," I tell him. "And . . . thanks."

"You too." He sighs. "I guess we both have our work cut out for us."

"I guess so," I say, thinking of Rynn as I know he's thinking of Ben.

He pats my shoulder as he wishes me goodnight and heads back through the dark to the cabins.

I should follow him. My window for sleeping is getting smaller by the second, and I know I'll regret all this pensive fire staring come morning. But my thoughts are moving so quickly, not even a questionably large dose of melatonin could lull them to sleep right now. I let myself stay wrapped in the embrace of the fire a moment longer. I take a sip of hot chocolate, grimace as I learn it's turned cold, and set the mug down by my feet.

Fitz is probably right about Ally not being inherently better than me. But the fact remains that she's one in a long list of people who have left me. Every time it happened—Rynn, my mom, Ally, Rynn again—I told myself it was just a blip, a moment to get through, and that once the moment passed, so could the feelings. They all add up to a pile teetering so high, I didn't know how to see past it anymore. But with Fitz's words ringing in my ears, it occurs to me that I've been telling my story all wrong, handing control to all the wrong people. That maybe the only way to tell this particular story is to live through it, piece by piece, on my own.

And, pulling out my phone to text Ally, I can't help but think it's high time I start doing exactly that.

20

TeleFanHour [13 hours ago]: THAT FINALE THOUGH!!! Will we ever be okay again? Sources say no.

AllysonHendricksOfficial [2 days ago]: Telephone Hour will always have such a special place in my heart. I treasured the years I spent playing Artis, and I'll always be so grateful to the fans who loved her with me. I can't believe how lucky I am to have filmed this last scene where Artis and Hemilia FINALLY end up together at last with my love @BeccaWallis. Grateful doesn't even begin to cover it.

It's goodbye to Telephone Hour, but it's not goodbye to y'all and it's not goodbye to Artis . . . stay tuned for an exciting announcement soon!

TeleFanHour: TUNED, girl!!!! Can't wait to hear what you're doing next!

BeccaWallis [47 minutes ago]: Unreal ending to an unreal journey. I'm forever grateful to the people who made this show happen and the people who loved it. But it's not quite over . . . @AllysonHendricksOfficial and I are SO excited to announce our spinoff show, HANG UP, which will follow Artis and Hemilia on their future space adventures. After years of pining both on set and in real life, I can't believe Hemilia and I both get the girl. I can't wait to see you all next fall for more space adventures!

GlindaWithAnI: AHHHHH A WHOLE SHOW WITH THE TWO OF YOU???? ALL MY DREAMS ARE COMING TRUE

EmmaHansen: WOW I can't wait!!

AllysonHendricksOfficial: love you, love our characters, love this life we get <3

RachelWesterly: COUPLE GOALS. So happy to see you happy after everything you've been through

NicolePotts: if by "been through" you mean having an affair . . .

HannahBaker: seriously. you're both so inspiring

AN EARLY-MORNING MIST CURLS OFF THE GRASS. I sigh, breathing in the sweetness of the cool morning air, and it refuels the strength I felt last night. Waking up in time to meet Ally here, it was easy to lose my willpower. All I could think about was the way her anger sliced through me yesterday. But

I'm not here to yell, or beg her followers for my side of the story, or even to drag a half-hearted apology out of her. I'm here to claim the next step of this story as my own.

She's waiting for me by the tallest pine tree in the middle of the field, just like I asked her. The morning light sinks into the air around us, brushing everything over with the palest gold. It's almost romantic—the soft-lit dew, the pale first rays of sunlight, the birdsong awakening in the branches. But I'm finally ready to let my feelings stand on their own two tottering toddler legs. I don't need the trappings of the story to dictate how I feel about it anymore. I'm here to write my own ending.

"I'm not sure why I'm here," she says. Her back is propped up against the pine tree, arms folded tight. "If you want to yell at me more, you could wait until a more reasonable hour."

A flicker of anger rears its head in my chest, but I force myself to breathe until it settles again. I'm not here to yell.

"Remember when we bought that sweater?" I ask instead, nodding to the thin white sweater she has on. I sink to the grass, dew soaking through my pajama bottoms, and cross my legs. "It was almost as early as it is now."

She bites her lip the way she does when she's fighting off a smile. "This hour is so much more reasonable when you're *still up*. For getting up, it's sick and wrong."

I look up at her, letting our eyes meet. "I'll never forget the way you begged the saleswoman to open early."

We'd been up all night—one of those magical first nights together in our early days of long distance—and after a late walk through her neighborhood that turned into an early-morning bakery crawl, we realized too late that we had locked ourselves out of her apartment. With her parents already off to work, her only hope of being ready for her rehearsal that day was buying a sweater to cover the frosting stain on the T-shirt she'd worn the day before.

"She was so nice," Ally says, sitting to match my posture. Our knees are almost touching, and I let myself lean forward to bump against her. It's a soft friendliness, and even though touching her tugs at the familiar ache in my chest, it doesn't hurt as searingly as it used to. I'm starting to see the way through it.

"I'm sorry," I say. "I wanted to tell you before you go. I'm sorry I posted it. It was vindictive and petty, and I shouldn't have done it."

Ally nods slowly, once. I don't need her forgiveness or for her to return the apology, but I can't deny that it would be nice to hear all the same.

"I'm sorry," she says, and I exhale. "For all of it. Shit. I'm so, so sorry." She tips her face into her hands, releasing a long sigh before lifting her head. "I should've handled everything so differently. I'm sorry."

It all just feels so . . . underwhelming. Almost four years of a relationship, one that lasted through long distance and fame. The culmination of a breakup that gripped the internet from its sudden debut to its shocking cheating scandal twist. It all ends with a soft-spoken apology one random summer morning. When we started dating, everyone assumed we'd hold hands on the playground for a few days and then move on to the next crush. When that didn't happen—when we stuck by each other through three-quarters of school—I thought our love story would be one for the ages. A starry-eyed tale about beating the odds, building a life no one expected, and spending my days on Ally's arm.

But here our story is, fizzling out into nothing.

Our eyes meet, and we burst out laughing. It's half-genuine, half-awkward desperation to break the tension somehow. Mercifully, it works.

"Do you think we'll ever . . ." Ally swallows, and for one terrifying moment, I'm afraid she's going to ask to get back together. It's what I'd have done anything for mere weeks ago, but now the thought fills me with dread. "Do you think we'll ever be friends again?"

She looks down at her fingernails, sleek pink but bitten to stubs. I reach out and squeeze her fingers.

"I hope so," I say softly. "I miss being friends."

The silent understanding passes between us that it'll take time, that it might never happen, that we might never find our way back to the ease of the friendship we once had. But we also might. For now, that's enough.

"Me too."

"Thank you," I say again, this time for more than the sliver of conversation we just had. This time, it's for everything I don't know how to put into words she'll understand. Thanks for being my first love. Thanks for our story.

Thanks for letting me go.

I stand, brushing away the grass that clings to my pajamas. "I should get ready for the day."

"You mean that's not your final look?" she asks with a grin.

I roll my eyes at her. The whole moment feels awash with nostalgia. The shock and the heartbreak and the mourning are fading into the distance, misted over with the knowledge that this is right. I bid goodbye to the girl I thought would be the love of my life, and I walk back up the path with a lightness I haven't felt in years.

THE MORNING IS A BLUR. TWYLA CRIES WHEN ALLY leaves, which I can hardly judge her for given how much I sobbed the last time she left me. I shuffle from class to class, from dramatic fight to stony dramatic silence, all while exchanging looks with Fitz that clearly communicate a certain *what the fuck* vibe I love to bring around with me these days.

I take my much-needed afternoon break in the empty office. I let the ancient couch swallow me whole and dedicate myself to staring at the ceiling. It's not exactly the meditative mindfulness that has been recommended to me by countless articles on improving one's mental health, all of which I've heartily ignored, but I'm too emotionally wrung out to do anything else right now.

My phone buzzes with yet another notification from the family group chat, which has been relentless all week. All summer if I'm being honest. I move to ignore it, contemplating silencing the chat entirely, when I see Lacey's name lighting up my screen. And all I can think about is the way she kept trying to meet my gaze in the car on the drive up here that day they dropped me off.

And before I realize what I'm doing, I'm calling her.

Because I'm not the only person Mom left.

She picks up on the first ring. "Hey-o!"

"Do you have time to talk?" I ask, surprised by how thick my voice is with the promise of tears.

Lacey must hear them because she immediately says, "Of course. Just give me a second to find a place to—AH! Oh god, that spider was as big as my head."

"Are you camping in Australia?"

"Just in the land of nightmares."

"The land of hyperbole, more like it."

Teasing her makes me feel better, but she's expecting a talk now. And if I'm being honest with myself, I still want one too. I listen to the rustle of her finding a place to sit, and then she says, "What's going on?"

"Do you ever feel like no one will ever love us?"

"You mean because Mom left?" Lacey says, so quickly it makes me feel dumb. We could've been having this conversation for years. We could've been therapisting each other about this since it happened. Hell, we could've been going to actual therapy too. But ignoring my feelings was so much easier. How was I supposed to know they were only in hiding, spending their time bulking up so that they could come back stronger than ever?

"Yeah," I tell Lacey. "But, like, add Ally and Rynn to my list, too."

"Ally sucks," Lacey says. "And Rynn? Wait, not Rynn Walsh?"

"Yeah." I fill her in on everything that's happened since she dropped me off. Fighting with Rynn. Finding out Ally cheated. Kissing Rynn. Being dumped by Rynn. She gasps and coos at all the right moments and makes sounds of indignant outrage that make me feel more seen than a billion of my defenders in Ally's comments section. I can't believe I've been denying myself this simple pleasure of confiding in my sister for years.

"Ally SUCKS," Lacey says again, her tone this time underlining it and setting it in bold. "I can't believe she cheated and let you find out via tabloids. Who the hell does that?"

"Yeah, it was pretty bad," I say. "And then she showed up here, and I had no idea what to do."

"And what was that last post about?" Lacey asks. "I mean, that was messy. You gotta get it together and take it down."

"I definitely messed up with the post," I admit.

"You could've popped a draft of that caption into the group chat before you posted it," Lacey says. "The one you've been ignoring all summer. We could help you."

"Sorry." I wince.

"It's okay," Lacey says. "I'm glad you called. I've been trying to have this exact conversation for years, you know."

"I do," I admit. "And it was the best. I'm sorry I stopped it from happening for so long."

"It's the curse of the oldest sister," Lacey says, and I can hear her shaking her head. "Thanks for calling. I have to get back to lunch or we'll never make it to our campsite and Dad will sacrifice me to the spiders."

"Your choice to go," I tease.

"Next year I'm bringing you so we can sacrifice you to the spiders instead," she says lovingly, and hangs up on me. I grin as I tuck my phone back into my pocket and force myself out of the couch's clutches. Lacey might come with all the grace of blunt force trauma, but only she can get me to laugh at my own problems. And she's right. I need to get it together. Even though it's been screenshotted so many times it might as well be tattooed on my forehead forever, I delete the post. Taking it down feels so much more powerful than giving in to the gossip spiral that was just looking for more fuel ever did.

I type out a quick caption. An apology to Ally for blasting her unnecessarily, an apology for shattering my privacy and hers, and an acknowledgment. *I'm going back to living my story instead of letting others tell it. Thank you to everyone who's listened.*

And before I post it, I pop my first draft into the group chat for approval.

When I swing my legs off the couch at the end of my break and force myself to slump back to my group, I feel lighter than I have all summer. There's just one thing still weighing heavy on my mind. I wish, desperately, that I could tell Rynn about all of this. She's come to be the one I trust most with the softest parts of my heart, and after having spent the summer unwinding myself for her, it feels wrong to keep this from her. But I also have no idea how she'd react to any of this. The thought terrifies me. I've already hurt her enough. The last thing I want to do is hurt her more—or lose her for good.

As if she hears my thoughts, which at this point seems likely, I swing open the office door to find her standing there.

"Oh," she says when my eyes catch hers. "Sorry, I didn't realize I was—"

"You're good," I say quickly. "I was just leaving."

She nods, her eyes somehow looking past me even though I'm staring right into them.

"Are you okay?" I ask. My own desire to confide in her is long gone, replaced with concern at the tightness in her jaw.

She gives a curt nod. "Yeah. Weird day, I guess."

"For sure." I have no idea what else to add. It's clear she doesn't want to talk to me, and yearn as I might to pull her into my arms and let her spill her troubles onto my shoulder, I don't want to push against her boundaries. I settle for stepping back to hold the door open for her. "Have a good break."

"Thanks," she murmurs. We cross paths in the doorway, and I walk away from her even as every muscle in my body aches for me to stay.

The Dads from Mamma Mia

LACEY: Dont forget to text us your new draft!!

IVY: How about you focus on surviving the hike

Then we can talk about my love life

LACEY: I can walk and read!!!!! Send draft!!!!!

I'm very good at love life-ing

IVY: WE KNOW

Ivy renamed the group chat: The Dynamos

—⚘—

I GRIN AS I TUCK MY PHONE INTO MY SHORTS POCKET. I never thought admitting to my sister that my whole life is falling apart would result in anything but embarrassment. To find help instead? No one is more shocked than me. With their support behind me, I uploaded the post as soon as they approved my draft.

The campgrounds are alive with the sound of morning free play. I should be helping Fitz with soccer game supervision, but when I told him my plan, he was so relieved he told me to go right now.

I sigh as I approach the main office, where Ms. P appears to be engaged in a full-on fight with the wizened desktop she does all the camp admin work on. I should've asked her to help with the Twyla-Nessa rivalry from the beginning. My pride got in the way of solving the problem and made things worse for the kids. It's time I fixed that.

I slip into the main office, comforted by its familiar cozy smell of coffee and chocolate.

"Thank goodness you're here," Ms. P mutters, shoving herself away from the computer. "I need a break from this thing."

"I need your help with something," I tell her, staring down at my shoes to hide the heat flooding my cheeks. There's nothing embarrassing about needing help, I remind myself, but I can't help feeling like a failure as I admit this to Ms. P.

She makes her way to the couch and gestures for me to join her. I sink into the cushions next to her, because these cushions give no other option, and fix my gaze on my knees.

"What's going on?" Ms. P asks. "If you're here to plead your case about the musical—"

"No," I say, wincing. As if it wasn't hard enough to admit my failures without being reminded of all the other ways I've failed at camp this year. The musical. Rynn. The emotional casualties I've managed to leave in my wake have piled so high, you'd think I was trying to ruin everything on purpose. "I am really sorry about—"

"I know," Ms. P says, her tone mercifully kind. She sits, staring me down, not with anger but with the clear expectation that it's my turn to talk, to tell her what I'm doing here.

"It's about two of my campers," I tell her. "Twyla and Nessa."

"The girls who got into a fight onstage?" Ms. P asks, and I nod. The whole story comes spilling out from there, how the tension between them has warped the whole social dynamic of our group so much that we still don't have a name.

"I wish you'd told me sooner," Ms. P says after I tell her about the argument leading up to the fight.

"Me too," I say, tracing my thumb along the lines of my palms. "I wanted to be able to do it on my own. To prove something. But that blew up in everyone's face."

"We're not here to prove ourselves as individuals," Ms. P says. "We're all on the same team. This job gets a whole lot better when we lean on each other. Collaboration not competition."

I nod. "I get that now."

It's what everyone's been trying to show me all along. Between Fitz begging me to get Ms. P involved and Rynn and Ben offering me help at every turn, everyone else has known we're on the same team. I'm the only one who thought I had to come out on top. And in doing so, I brought everyone down.

Yikes.

"It sounds like the girls need to talk it out," Ms. P says.

My eyes widen at the thought. "Are you sure? Them talking has historically not gone great."

Ms. P nods. "They need your help."

Two sixth graders who didn't have completely amazing communication skills? Unprecedented. My own words to Rynn flash through my mind. Because I've been in their shoes before, desperate to make my heart known but unable to translate the spiral of emotions constantly tearing through me into coherent thoughts, let alone words that could make sense to other people. And that ended with my best friendship evaporating into a puff of black smoke.

Twyla and Nessa came to camp so close. If they leave here not speaking, the world will be a worse place, I decide. Their worlds are better with each other in them.

"Okay," I tell Ms. P. "But will you help me help them?"

"Of course. Let's get them together, okay?" Ms. P pushes herself off the couch with both hands, which is the only way to escape the clutches of these cushions. "I'll give you some guidelines, but I think it should start with just you and them. They know you. If you need help, text me, okay?"

As I follow her to the field, Ms. P preps me with a few strategies. We track down the girls and bring them back to the main office.

They walk on opposite sides of me, not looking at each other. I catch sight of Twyla's face as I hold the main office door open for them, and the wild nervousness in her wide eyes almost bowls me over. They think they're in trouble. Ms. P said the conversation should feel like a safe space where they're able to express their feelings openly and kindly, and walking in with a fear of repercussions isn't going to help. I follow them in and decide to improvise.

"Who wants some hot chocolate?" I ask, flipping on the water heater. "I know it's a billion degrees out, but I want marshmallows, and if I make one more s'more this summer, I think I might melt."

Twyla giggles, a tense sound that comes more from her own nerves than my vivacious sense of humor. "Sure."

"Thanks," Nessa says.

"Y'all aren't in trouble," I reassure them as I empty chocolate powder packets into three mugs. "I just need your help with something."

I pour the hot water into the three powder-filled mugs and smother each with a handful of mini marshmallows.

"With what?" Twyla asks.

"You came here really close friends," I remind them as I set two mugs onto the coffee table and go back to the counter for mine. "I don't think my heart would ever recover if that wasn't true anymore when we left."

I let my words sink in as I sit cross-legged on the floor across from them, my mug steaming between my hands. I'm too sweaty to bring myself to take a sip yet, but the warmth against my fingers and the chocolaty smell wafting up to me offer enough comfort.

"Because of your breakup with Allyson?" Twyla asks.

I snort. "Believe it or not, some things are not about Allyson."

Twyla stares at me with a look that makes it clear she has elected to *not*.

I take a deep breath, remembering what Rynn suggested about being vulnerable with the kids. *Just be real with them.* It sounds so easy, but I feel like I'm standing on the precipice of an ocean, towering waves hiding sweeping currents, being told to just swim across.

"I'm actually thinking of a different breakup," I say, and their eyes go wide. "A friend breakup. I was about your age, and my best friend and I decided to stop being friends. And honestly? I've regretted that day ever since."

Twyla and Nessa exchange looks, and for the first time I see a flicker of the closeness that existed steadfastly between them on the first day.

"Friendship stuff can be as hard as romantic breakups, but people generally don't talk about it in the same way, so it can be tough to learn how to handle it," I go on. "Sometimes I think if my friend and I had been able to find the words to explain what was bothering us, we'd have been able to work through it. And then maybe we could still be friends. I know my life would be better with her in it."

I take in their reactions, trying to ignore how much the advice I'm giving them still applies to Rynn and me. But we've never been able to find the words. And our issues run deeper than the casting of a summer camp musical.

"That's what I want for you two," I say, reaching an upturned palm toward each of them. "How about we spend a little time trying to find the words?"

The two exchange glances again. Twyla nods.

"Okay," Nessa says, her voice watery. "Can I start? I think I have some."

I nod encouragingly. "Just keep in mind this isn't a place we're going to accuse each other or keep fighting. We're putting our feelings into words. Sometimes understanding where someone else is coming from helps a lot."

"I made up a fake boyfriend because I was embarrassed," Nessa says, the words coming out so fast that they trip over each other into a big pile at the finish line.

"What do you mean?" Twyla asks.

"You always are so good at everything," Nessa says. "I was really nervous coming to camp. You're the only person I know here, and you never have a hard time making friends or fitting in or anything. I just wanted people to like me, too."

I nod. "Being in a romantic relationship comes with so much social capital. And that's so, so messed up. Whether or not someone is in a relationship has absolutely nothing to do with their worth as a person, and thinking otherwise is so dangerous. You're such a good friend, Ness, and whether or not you have a boyfriend has nothing to do with how much people will like you."

I surprise myself with how clear my tone makes it that I feel these words deeply. But it's true. The cultural cachet that came with being in a relationship kept me with Ally longer than I would've ever thought I'd stay together with someone who made me feel so small. And sure, the fact that she was a celebrity only exacerbated the feeling that being in a relationship with her gave me some kind of power, a position I'd lose if I let her go. But if the way we talk about dating has even sixth graders yearning for relationships and requited crushes not for love, but for the capital that comes with it, the story we're telling them about romance has gone wrong.

"I just thought it was what I had to do," Nessa says, staring at her upturned palms on her lap.

Twyla bursts into tears at Nessa's speech. Surprised, I track down a box of tissues and set them in front of her. She ignores them, mopping her face with her sleeve instead.

"I thought we were best friends," she sobs. "It hurt so much to find out you lied to me."

"Well, it hurt when you were mad something good happened to me," Nessa says, her tone rising. "Why couldn't you be happy for me when I got Wendy?"

"Remember, focus on how it made you feel," I say softly.

A thick silence settles over the coffee table. I take a long sip of my too-hot chocolate. It's the kind of silence that's busy with thinking, and I wait for it to bring itself to an end.

"I'm sorry," Twyla says at last. "I should've been happy for you. I was jealous."

"It's understandable to feel jealous of our friends sometimes," I tell her. "As long as we remember to listen to the part of us that's happy for them, too. Someone else's joy doesn't have to take away from your own."

Twyla nods, picking a goopy marshmallow from her mug and sucking it off her finger.

"I'm sorry too," Nessa said. "I should've been honest. About the fake boyfriend, and about the fact that I really did want Wendy."

The stillness that follows this is a sniffly one. I give them several minutes to process what's been said, and then softly clear my throat.

"So . . . what are we thinking? Did that help?"

I cross my fingers tightly against the still-hot side of my mug. If they're not ready to mend things after all that, I have truly no idea where to go from here.

But then Twyla nods. "Yeah."

"Friends?" Nessa asks, so softly it almost makes me cry.

"Friends," Twyla agrees.

They get up, not looking at each other still, and I know it will take a little while for the awkwardness between them to fully dissipate. But at least they're on the way. I tell them to go back to free play, and they bounce toward the door.

"That wasn't so hard, Counselor Ivy." Twyla pauses at the

door, turning to face me. "You were pretty good at finding the words. Maybe if you looked, you could find them for your friend, too."

"Maybe," I say softly, but she's gone before she can hear me.

WHEN I FOLLOW THE GIRLS TO THE FIELD TO RELIEVE Fitz from soccer supervision duty, I see Rynn standing by the goalpost, dabbing sweat from her forehead. I take a deep breath, the air heavy with the sweet smell of cut grass, and make my way down the hill to meet her.

"Hey," I say quietly, almost hoping she won't hear me.

She does, though she doesn't look at me. "Hi."

"Sorry about . . . the other day," I say. She looks at me now, her eyes unreadable. "I was upset and I lashed out. I shouldn't have been so unkind. I'm sorry."

"I'm sorry too," she says. "I should've gone about it differently."

"I'm sorry about the whole summer," I say. "You were right. I was trying to skip over grieving my relationship, and I shouldn't have pulled you into my mess. I think I'm moving past it now. For real this time."

I hover near her for a moment, hoping against hope, as she turns her gaze back to the soccer game.

"I should've said it differently, but what I said is still true," she says softly. "I don't want to be your secret rebound."

"You could never be." But I didn't come to push, I came to

apologize. And that's done, leaving me with nothing to do but go supervise something else.

As I turn to leave, she calls out.

"Ivy?"

I spin to face her, my teeth landing hard against my lower lip. "Yeah?"

"I can talk to Ms. P, let her know we can work together again," Rynn says. "I'm leaving soon anyway."

Her words slap against my eardrums, a shock roiling from the inside out.

"What do you mean?"

She rubs the back of her neck. "I decided to leave early. They only need me until the end of dress rehearsals, really. I have to . . ." She trails off, her eyes looking past me at the closed purple buds dotting the grass. "It's been a hard couple of days. Ally coming here, and I—I just have to get home."

"You can't leave." The words burst out of me before I have time to think about them. The thought of letting her slip quietly out of my life hurts too much to let it take root. This place may have started as my home, but over the years it's become hers. Neither I nor Ally should be able to take that from her.

She shakes her head. "I have to. But you should take over, as director."

It's a generous offer, and I can tell from the way she's looking at me that it's a genuine one. But I've made such a mess of things. Letting Rynn see this thing to the end is a small way to fix things, but it's the only way I have right now. Besides, I still can't accept that she's about to just . . . disappear. I have to find a way to stop her, to keep her here. If not for me, then for her, and for her relationship with this place we've both come to love.

"That's okay," I say. "You should get to do it on your terms. You were doing a better job than me."

"True," Rynn says with a wry grin, but I can't bring myself to return it.

٭

TO MY RELIEF, MY CAMPER GROUP STAYS RECONCILED. Nessa and Twyla hold hands on the way back to the cabin from dinner, and I have to restrain myself from physically cooing at how adorable it is.

I practically crawl to my own bunk, exhausted from the weight of the day. Shepherding Twyla and Nessa through their friendship troubles feels like weeks ago. I can't believe that was just this morning.

I thud onto my mattress, expecting sleep to come quick, but my thoughts are too alive to succumb to dreams. I lie there, eyes screwed shut, thinking about love and what's next for me. My brain floods me with her bright eyes, the soft smell of her hair, and the taste of her smile against my lips, and my heart breaks all over again at this fresh onslaught of memories.

But it's not Ally I'm thinking of anymore.

It's Rynn.

22

A NIGHT FULL OF DREAMING OF RYNN, AND A MORN-
ing of daydreams. I know what she meant now, when she asked if
I was really over Ally. It's not just about not loving Ally anymore—
maybe a piece of me always will. People say that about first loves.

But my heart is wide-open now and ready to embrace someone new. Someone exactly Rynn-sized, ideally.

Lucky for me, all my daydreaming has dredged up a recent
memory. Rynn in the kitchen, flour dotting her face alongside
her freckles.

And I know how to show her that I'm ready to be all-in, to
give her my whole heart. No less than she deserves.

I have just a handful of hours left to put it together.

Twyla is an easy recruitment, and she and Nessa get the
rest of the group on board. We only have until the end of dress
rehearsal, so we sneak to the amphitheater early to set every-

thing up. It has to go perfectly. Nessa sets about sweeping the stage, which is patently unnecessary, but she spends the whole time muttering "has to be perfect" to herself, so I'm not in a position to disagree. Twyla sets up the audio system, and I "supervise" her, a move that consists mostly of worrying over her shoulder because I don't actually know how to use the audio system.

Fitz leads the rest of our group into the theater as we're preparing the choreography. Nessa and Twyla take over teaching them the moves we came up with. Sammy and Ella turn out to be incredible dancers, and they add a waltz situation that sends them twirling around the stage.

Footsteps rustle against the pine needle–laden path, and we scatter off the stage, the kids squealing as they bump into each other in their frantic rush. They tuck themselves away just in time.

Rynn, Celia, and Ben file in with their groups, directing them to the backstage area where they're supposed to get ready for the performance. I swallow thickly when I see her. My first thought is that she's heartbreakingly beautiful. The midmorning light sinks into her hair, bringing out its golden undertones. Her eyes light up as she laughs at some joke Ben makes, and they could outshine any star in the sky. But she has a duffel bag slung over her shoulder, bulging with everything she brought here this summer, ready to disappear.

Then I blink, and Rynn, Celia, and Ben have taken their seats in the front row.

That's our cue.

I signal to Twyla, who presses the button that starts the song up. More specifically, her song. Rynn's song.

The first notes fill the air, and it takes Rynn a moment to recognize the tune and turn around. When she does, her jaw drops as she registers me on the stage, mic in hand. She bursts into laughter as I start singing the lyrics she penned. The ones she wanted so badly to hear come to life.

My group of campers stomps onto the stage around me, breaking out into the choreographed number, just like we practiced. Just like Rynn said she wanted. A gesture just for her, one she didn't have to plan or prep or make happen herself. All she has to do is throw her head back and laugh as we strike our ridiculous ending pose.

But the song itself isn't enough. I know that. She hasn't been waiting to test my vocals; she's wanted to know that I'm ready to put her first. Without pushing her into the plants whenever someone walks by.

My heart hammers as I wipe my sweaty palms against the sequins of the skirt I picked out for the occasion. I lift the mic to my lips, and across the amphitheater, Rynn sits up straighter.

"I just wanted to tell you all that Counselor Rynn is the best," I say, starting at how loudly my voice echoes through the space. "I'm proud to call her my friend and I'm glad I get to have her in my life."

A cheer goes out from my campers, and Rynn's group joins in, whooping as they crowd around their counselor.

"The other counselors are great too," I add, finding Fitz's smiling eyes in the audience.

I leave it at that. Probably Ms. P wouldn't be thrilled if I announced my romantic overtures in front of all the campers. Besides, I don't want to force Rynn into a corner. The public nature of this is just to show her that I'm all-in on *us,* that I don't want to hide anymore, not to pressure her into giving me an answer.

Even with the bit of discretion I manage to work in, I know they'll talk about this later. I might as well be blowing wind straight into the rumor mill, giving it so much to churn through, but I don't care. I'm done worrying about the stories other people will tell about me. I can't live a life worth living if I spend it in the shadows, away from where anyone might notice anything I do.

Rynn is worth stepping into the spotlight for.

She watches me as I set the mic back on its stand (mic drops are *expensive*), but I can't read her expression. She gazes up at me, and her lips are quirked at the corners. The duffel has fallen to her feet. But I'm too scared to read into that. Duffels are heavy. I can't expect her to carry it around all day. So she set it down. Doesn't make it a visual metaphor.

Ms. P joins us, and I run offstage with my group. Once we're onto the dirt sidelines, they cheer, pulling me into a group hug.

"You did it for sure," Twyla says.

"Like you did for us," Nessa adds.

I squeeze their shoulders tighter for a second before letting them go. "Couldn't have done it without my backup dancers."

"Hey, that's a good group name," Nessa says.

"It's perfect," Twyla agrees. "Show of hands for the Backup Dancers."

And when every single one of them throws their fingers to the sky, I could cry.

PETER PAN HAS THE LONGEST RUN TIME IN THE HIS-tory of musical theater.

I mean, I have no idea if that's true, but it sure feels like it is. I couldn't find Rynn before Ms. P came into the amphitheater to announce that everyone needed to get to their places as she started letting the audience in. I had to guide my group to their places and run to help Celia with the music cues. Rynn, plugged into her headset, is busy running the whole show.

Which means my impromptu musical number and I have been left to stew.

That dang ship can't get off the stage fast enough.

Finally, finally, the kids take their bows. They're met with raucous applause from the audience. My skin itches so much as everyone takes their sweet time getting out of the theater that I check my arms multiple times for hives.

But at last, the space is empty.

The sun is nearing the horizon, casting everything in a pink glow that filters through the trees onto the stage. I step onto its smooth stone surface, scanning the pit for Rynn. I find her sitting on the edge of the stage, legs swinging in the space below, headset lying by her side. Duffel bag nowhere to be seen.

I slide down next to her, our fingers a breath away from each other.

"Ms. P told me the show went great," Rynn says with a smile. "I mean, some of the lines were a little wonky, but a lot of parents told her it seemed like the kids had a great summer."

"I hope they did," I say. "They can always fix the wonky lines in tomorrow's performance."

"I hope it means there's a camp for us to come back to next summer."

My heart might as well grab a jump rope and start singing "Miss Mary Mack" for the number of beats it's jumping. "Us?"

"That was quite the song," she says, grinning as she shoots me a sideways glance. "I missed you, Raines."

"I missed you too," I say. "The past week has been hell without you."

She slips her hand into mine. "I don't just mean the last week. I mean the last five years."

I open my mouth to start singing, because I am who I am and not even the most romantic of moments can take that from me, but she sees my intention and laughs before I can start.

"I'm serious. I missed you every day. For five years, I thought of you every single day."

"I did too. And I'm ready to be all-in," I say. "No more Ally. No more hiding. Just us. I mean. No pressure. I just—if you—"

She cuts me off wordlessly, her lips pressing to mine. It takes me off guard, sudden like an earthquake, except instead of tearing me apart, she's rattled all the pieces back into place. It's soft this time, building slowly, full of her smile and her minty lip balm and the promise of more to come.

23

I THOUGHT I WAS READY.

Now, standing among the chaos of an overflooded lot full of triple-parked cars, a zillion duffel bags smacking passersby in the face, and parents shouting to their kids, I know the truth: I. Am. Not. Ready. No amount of summertime training with Ms. P and advice from Rynn could ever have prepared me for this moment, for the reality of handing my campers back to their parents.

Twyla's arms squeeze tight around my waist, and I grin at her and Nessa as they crowd around me.

"Thanks for saving our friendship," Nessa says. Her pinkie is interlocked with Twyla's, a familiar sight that teases a teary smile out of me.

"Seriously," Twyla says, glancing back at the gray Subaru waiting for them in the parking lot. "We're carpooling home, so it would've been seriously awkward if you didn't."

Nessa smacks her arm, and the two take off, laughing. I

move on to hugging Wally and Elliott goodbye, knowing that all these kids are taking a piece of my heart with them.

It probably takes hours to empty the tightly packed driveway, but I blink and everyone is gone. Back home, spilling memories onto their parents, this summer a story they can't wait to tell.

Rynn slides her hand into mine, her fingers warm and clammy with midday summer sweat.

"Ready for the last day of summer?" she asks, squeezing my fingers.

I shake my head. "Definitely not."

"Let's not waste it then," she says, her lips curving upward as she pulls me into them. I lose myself in their softness, in the easy way they promise more tomorrow. Even though we'll be splitting off to our respective homes, flung a little too far away from each other, I know just as certainly that I never want to go another day without her in my life.

In truth, I can't say for sure what the rest of my story holds. I just know I'm excited to write it.

Myself.

Acknowledgments

Some say writing is lonely, but not the way I do it (by complaining loudly and incessantly to all my loved ones). As usual, this means I reached the end of this book filled with gratitude for the people who helped me along the journey.

Thank you so much to my incredible agent, Penny Moore, for making this all happen. I feel so lucky and grateful always to have you in my corner.

Kelsey Horton—thank you so much for your belief in me and my stories, and for always having the insight to make them better. I'm forever grateful to be doing this work with you.

Thanks to everyone at Delacorte Press and Penguin Random House for all your work in bringing this book together. Tamar Schwartz, Tim Terhune, Colleen Fellingham, Megan Shortt, and Trisha Previte—thank you for making this story what it is.

I owe my very deepest thanks and love always to the coven. Sonia Hartl, Annette Christie, Kelsey Rodkey, Susan Lee, Rachel Solomon—you really are heroes, and I couldn't do this (or anything, probably) without you. Much thanks also to Marisa Kanter and Carlyn Greenwald for your guidance through writing this book and for your kind patience as we all wait for Summer Auriane to come back.

Thank you to Jack Filsinger and Robert Jewell for reading the very worst version of this book and politely pretending to like it so that I would stop having a mental breakdown about revisions.

My work as a teacher makes writing possible in more ways than one. Thank you infinitely to Luke for your brilliance, patience, and jokes (except when I'm about to take a sip of water, in which case I'm actually quite ungrateful). Thank you to our students for reminding me to love Nessa (sorry she's not included in the dedication for this book. She is, in my defense, not a dog). Thank you to Karen for being the teacher who taught me.

Shout-out to Erin for always being down to stop what you're doing when I ask you to look at Sammy. Your partnership, both in documenting Sammy's cuteness and in life, is everything.

My most heartfelt thanks to all the readers who have supported this journey. Without you, none of it is possible—thank you.

About the Author

AURIANE DESOMBRE is a middle-school teacher and the author of *I Think I Love You, The Sister Split,* and *I Love You S'more.* She holds an MA in English Literature and an MFA in Creative Writing for Children & Young Adults. She lives in Los Angeles with her dog, Sammy, who is a certified bad boy.

AURIANEDESOMBRE.COM